Snowball's
Chance

Snowball's
Chance

John Reed

ROOF BOOKS
NEW YORK

ISBN: 1-931824-05-3
Library of Congress Catalog Card No.: 2002107548
Book Design by Deborah Thomas.

Roof Books are distributed by
Small Press Distribution
1341 Seventh Avenue
Berkeley, CA. 94710-1403.
Phone orders: 800-869-7553
spdbooks.org

 This book is made possible, in part, with public
funds from the New York State Council on the Arts,
a state agency.
NYSCA

ROOF BOOKS
are published by
Segue Foundation
303 East 8th Street
New York, NY 10009
segue.org

Foreword: The Fable of the Weasel

Snowball's Chance takes its intriguing departure from *Animal Farm*, and set me thinking again about Orwell. These days I can't get through almost any page of Orwell without a shudder, though in my teens I often had the Penguin selection of his essays in my pocket. I'd learned to loathe *Animal Farm* earlier at my prep school, Heatherdown, where any arguments for socialism would be met with brays of "and some are more equal than others" by my school mates.

Some writers admired in adolescence stay around for the rest of the journey, perennial sources of refreshment and uplift: P.G. Wodehouse, Stanley Weyman, H.L. Mencken, Flann O'Brien, to name but four I'd be glad to find in any bathroom. Now, why can Mencken delight me still, while the mere sight of a page of Orwell carries me back to memories of England and of British-ness at full disagreeable stretch: philistine, vulgar, thuggish, flag-wagging?

Maybe the answer comes with the flag-wagging. Mencken made terrible errors of political judgement. Like Orwell he could be a lout. Both men's prose has excited awful imitators. But Mencken was a true outsider. Orwell wasn't. To step into Mencken-land is to be lured down a thousand unexpected pathways, with firecrackers of wit exploding under one's feet. Contradicting Thomas Love Peacock's famous jibe at land-scapers, even on the twentieth tour of the Mencken estate there are surprises. I don't feel that, trundling through Orwell Country. It gets less alluring with each visit. What once seemed bracing, now sounds boorish. How quickly one learns to loathe the affectations of plain bluntishness. The man of conscience turns out to be a whiner, and of course a snitch, an informer to the secret police, Animal Farm's resident weasel.

When Orwell's secret denunciations surfaced a few years

ago, there was a medium-level commotion. Then, with the publication of Peter Davison's maniacally complete twenty-volume collected Orwell, the topic of Orwell as government snitch flared again, with more lissome apologies for St. George from the liberal/left and bellows of applause from cold warriors, taking the line that if Orwell, great hero of the non-Communist left, named names, then that provides moral cover for all the Namers of Names who came after him.

Those on the non-Com left rushed to shore up St. George's reputation. Some emphasized Orwell's personal feeling toward Kirwan. The guy was in love. Others argued that Orwell was near death's door, traditionally a time for confessionals. Others insisted that Orwell didn't really name names, and anyway (this was the late Ian Hamilton in the *London Review of Books*), "he was forever making lists,"—a fishing log—a log of how many eggs his hens laid; so why not a snitch list?

"Orwell named no names and disclosed no identities," proclaimed Christopher Hitchens, one of Orwell's most ecstatic admirers. Clearly, Orwell did both, as in "Parker, Ralph. Underground member and close FT [fellow traveler?] Stayed on in Moscow. Probably careerist."

Apologists for Orwell sometimes suggest this was a sort of parlor game between Rees and Orwell, playful scribbles that somehow ended up with Kirwan. The facts are otherwise. Orwell carefully and secretly remitted to Celia Kirwan, an agent of the IRD or Information Research Department, a list of the names of persons on the left who he deemed security risks, as Communists or fellow travelers. The IRD was lodged in the British Foreign Office but in fact over-seen by the Secret Intelligence Service, otherwise known as MI6.

Kirwan, with whom Orwell had previously had some sort of liaison, visited Orwell in Cranham on March 29, 1949. She reported to the Department the next day that she "had discussed some aspects of our work with him in great confidence, and he was delighted to learn of them." Case Officer Lt. Colonel Sheridan annotated this report.

On April 6, a week later, Orwell wrote to his friend Richard Rees, asking him to find and send "a quarto notebook with a pale bluish cardboard cover" containing "a list of list of crypto-Communists and fellow-travellers which I want to bring up to date." Rees duly dispatched the notebook and Orwell wrote on May 2 to Kirwan, "I enclose a list with about 35 names," modestly adding that "I don't suppose it will tell your friends anything they don't know," and reflecting that, although the IRD probably had tabs on the subjects already, "it isn't a bad idea to have people who are probably unreliable listed."

Reviewing this sequence in the *London Review of Books* early in 2000, Perry Anderson emphasized some important points. Orwell knew the destination of the list, and "was very anxious to keep the list hidden." It remains thus. Though 99 names from the notebook are displayed in Vol. XX of Orwell's Collected Works, with another 36 withheld by the editor for fear of libel, the list of 35 remains a state secret, lodged in the Foreign Office archives.

Those secret advisories to an IRD staffer had consequences. Blacklists usually do. No doubt the list was passed on in some form to American intelligence that made due note of those listed as fellow travelers and duly proscribed them under the McCarran Act.

Hitchens has written softly of Orwell's "tendresse" for Kirwan, as though love rather than loyalty led him forward. Against the evidence under our noses he insists Orwell "wasn't interested in unearthing heresy or in getting people fired or in putting them under the discipline of loyalty oath." Although as opposed to the mellow tendresse for secret agent Kirwan, he had "an acid contempt for the Communists who had betrayed their cause and their country once before and might do so again."

Here Orwell would surely have given a vigorous nod. Orwell's defenders claim that he was only making sure the wrong sort of person wasn't hired by the Foreign Office to write essays on the British ways of life. But Orwell made it clear to the IRD he was identifying people who were "unreliable" and who, worming their way into organizations like the British Labor Party, "might be able to do enormous mischief." Loyalty was the issue, and it's plain enough from his annotations that Orwell thought that Jews, blacks, and homosexuals had an inherent tropism towards treachery to the values protected by the coalition of patriots including himself and the IRD. G.D.H. Cole, Orwell noted, was "shallow," a "sympathizer" and also a "diabetic."

There seems to be general agreement by Orwell's fans left and right, to skate gently over these Orwellian suspicions of Jews, homosexuals, and blacks, also the extreme ignorance of his assessments, reminiscent of police intelligence files the world over. Of Paul Robeson Orwell wrote, "very anti-white. [Henry] Wallace supporter." Only a person who instinctively thought all blacks were anti-white could have written this piece of stupidity. One of Robeson's indisputable features, consequent upon his intellectual disposition and his connections with the Communists, was that he was most emphatically not "very anti-white," Ask the Welsh coal miners for whom Robeson campaigned.

If any other postwar intellectual was suddenly found to have written mini-diatribes about blacks, homosexuals, and Jews, we can safely assume that subsequent commentary would not have been forgiving. There was certainly no forgivenness for Mencken. But Orwell gets a pass. "Deutscher [Polish Jew]," "Driberg, Tom. English Jew," "Chaplin, Charles (Jewish?)." No denunciations from the normally sensitive Norman Podhoretz.

When someone becomes a saint, everything is mustered as testimony to his holiness. So it is with St. George and his list. Thus, in 1998, when the list became an issue, we have fresh endorsement of all the cold war constructs as they were shaped in the immediate postwar years, when the cold war coalition from right to left signed on to fanatical anti-Communism. The IRD, disabled in the seventies by a Labor Foreign Minister on the grounds it was a sinkhole of right-wing nuts, would have been pleased.

Orwell's *Animal Farm* is a powerful fable, though as I've noted, in my experience, the effect of the fable has mostly been to deride the utopian impulse. Orwell as Weasel is a powerful fable too, as powerful as the awful saga of betrayal conducted by that other Cold War saint, Ignacio Silone. "The Fable of the Weasel" is cautionary, not least about defenders of Orwell's conduct. If they thought what he did was okay, or even better than okay, somehow an act of sublime bravery, should one not assume that they regard snitching against Traitors to the West as a moral duty too. We have been warned. John Reed's parody in *Snowball's Chance* warns us too, how the non-Com side plays on Orwell's very field.

Alexander Cockburn

Petrolia, California
July, 2002

I

THE OLD PIGS were dying. First, it was Dominicus—a secondary functionary who had given over his life to that rather crucial task of interpreting and graphing statistical data. He wore black-rimmed glasses and liked to sing opera as he sat at his desk—where, one drizzly afternoon, he collapsed into a plate of Camembert. By unanimous proclamation, he was named Animal Hero, First Class. The next pig to die was Napoleon himself. The great Berkshire boar. The father of all animals. Savior of equality, liberty, and freedom. He had died in a manner fit to his station—passing in his sleep, between sheets of Egyptian cotton (with an extremely high thread-count).

In commemorative tribute, a twelve-foot statue of Napoleon was erected outside the barnhouse, at the former site of Old Major's skull, for those who remembered Old Major, the pig who had started it all, and those days—those early, early days.

The statue was bronze—Napoleon wore his black coat and his leather leggings. Standing on his hind-legs, he puffed his pipe and looked to the horizon. Behind the statue, painted in white letters on the tar wall of the barn, was the single Commandment—*Most animals are equalish*. To the left of the Commandment, the verses of *Founding Father Napoleon* were painted in the same white letters. The poem, dedicated to the fallen leader, was authored by Minimus, who was known to be a pig with a poetic soul—

Napoleon taught us how to read.
Napoleon gives us grass and feed.
Napoleon shows us bread can rise,
With a swill o' swell guidance from the swine.

The pigs are a species of splendorous knowing,
But also of helping, and also of showing—
That the animals of the Manor Farm
Are the tippest-toppest animals anywhere! Gosh-darn!

So let's give a honk and a quack and a squeak!
An oink and a moo and a whinny and a peep!
Let's doodle-doo, let's snort, and let's baaa!
Let's give a bark and a hoot and a caaw!

Don't hold it back! You squeal and you neigh!
Napoleon, Napoleon, you're king amongst the hay!
Napoleon, Napoleon, we know you'll lead the way!
Napoleon, Napoleon, guide us everyday!

To further observe the accomplishments of the great Leader, the portrait of Napoleon, which surmounted the poem, was refreshed. Six pigeons, with a retouch of color, gave dimension to the white profile—under the tutelage of the pigs, the birds had acquired the skill of rendering.

In the year that followed, several more of the old-time swiners cast off their mortal coil. One would drown in the bathtub (through no fault of his own) when he found himself unable to get out. Another would fall victim to a swollen liver—downing his last mug of whiskey, he quietly moved on to the next life. Yet another would die of a patient torturer called cancer—fortunately, as he had long taken up

Napoleon's habit of enjoying a good pipe several times an hour, he was offered much consolation in his final months. All, heroes of the rebellion, were declared Animal Heroes, First Class.

The younger pigs filled their places well enough, it seemed, though they were a reserved generation—more aloof, and perhaps, more lenient. They were led by their elder, Squealer, who for years had been Napoleon's chief counselor. He was a pig who could wag his tail and tongue quite persuasively—so much so that in the end, he may have convinced even himself that he was a pig of the populace. Though he had been saying for years that rations were increasing, for the first time that anyone could remember (aside from the pigs, who were always firm in their conviction that things were always getting better) it seemed possible that the ration-bag was a little rounder—and noticeably so. When Squealer died, he himself had grown so fat that he was blinded by his own face. The cause of death, it was pronounced, was overwork.

In another first (or at least the first that anyone could remember), this pronouncement by the pigs was openly derided. At the posthumous awards presentation (Animal Hero, First Class), there were even a few stealthy hecklers—hooters and honkers. Squealer wasn't so terrible, after all—but surely, a pig who in his last days was pushed around in a wheelbarrow, as he could not even sustain his girth on four legs, was no pig who had, as it was claimed, died of "a lifetime of exertion." It would have taken old Squealer himself to explain that a pig buried in a piano case wasn't funny.

The last of the old pigs to take control was Minimus. He, like the others before him, was considered one of the original heroes of the rebellion. (And yet, his ascent was cause for much surprise, as aside from compose a few poems, nobody could accurately pinpoint what he had done.) Though robust, Minimus was quite advanced in years—and to address concerns that the next succession might be turbulent, Pinkeye, the most powerful, and incidentally, well-liked pig of the younger generation, was selected to fill the newly created position, Next Leader.

So Pinkeye kissed ducklings and lambs, as Minimus went about managing the farm. A silent Leader, Minimus was a mystery to be feared and respected. The dogs were loyal to his service, as were the other pigs, just as it had always been. And yet there was a new calm—unprecedented—a calm bespeaking, perhaps, a better future, or perhaps, the darkness of days to come.

It was one night—an average sort of normal May night— that there was an extra-extraordinary disturbance in the stalls. The moon low on the horizon, a figure had appeared at the gates. It was a strange figure—unfamiliar in his dark suit with pleated pants and a wide lapel. The animal (was it an animal?) walked on two feet, wore shoes and a brimmed hat, and carried a briefcase. A few steps behind him, a goat was similarly accoutered. (Was it a goat? Yes, it was a goat. Surely, a most sophisticated goat.)

The dog in attendance at the outer gate barked ferociously at the pair—though not many of the barn animals paid him much mind, as the dogs at the outer gate were particularly high-strung beasts, known to be incited to woof by causes so innocuous as moon shadows and silverfish. One of the cows, no doubt bolstered by the anonymity of night, belted out her exasperation at having been, once again, so rudely awoken—

"Shaaat-up!"

In actuality, however, the scene that took place at the outer gate was not nearly so common as the cow imagined—for although the cause of the shepherd's excitement was a stranger, and not a silverfish, after what seemed scarcely more than a few well-chosen words, the guard dog, having dropped to his forelegs, was backing away on his belly. Mouth closed, eyes wide, he lowered his head and tucked his tail under his haunches — as the briefcased pair, cutting elegant if foreboding silhouettes against the indigo sky, breached the outer gate with no more discussion.

From her perch in the hayloft, Norma the cat, who had been watching the moon through the chinks in the barn, was the single animal to witness the brief exchange. Norma, like most cats, was more interested in being a cat than a member of the Manor Farm. Yet she was an extremely personable creature — always playful. And, excepting those times she was lazing around in the shade while the other animals were huffing in the sun, she was widely appreciated.

"Sssssssss!" she hissed at the broken windowpane — her back arched, her claws extended, her hair on end.

This, as would be expected, immediately woke the rats, who endeavored to keep themselves well attuned to the cat. Seeing that Norma was nowhere near their nest (for there were nights when the feline, overly affable, chose from among them some unfortunate favorite to frolic to death), the rats scurried along the high beams to see for themselves what had caused such unease.

What the rats saw were the two figures — a goat, and now it could be discerned, a pig — crossing the hayfield to the barn.

The sheep too, arising, looked to the nearing comers. Nervously, they paced their stalls. "Ohhhh," they fretted anxiously —

"Shall we worry? Shall we worry?"

With that, the old donkey Benjamin woke. Benjamin was

the oldest animal on the farm (as old as yesterday itself, said some of the geese) and lowering his fourth leg, as donkeys sleep on three legs, he turned to a slat missing from the side of his stall—his eyes cynical and bitter as ever.

As the story went, long ago, Benjamin had suffered some disappointment, and maybe lost a friend, or two. And that was why he hardly spoke, except to utter an occasional—

"None of you have seen a donkey die, and none of you will."

This was said with an enormous remorse. And as he spoke, Benjamin would look at an animal as if he knew exactly where that animal was in his or her life. And the farm animals shuddered to look back at Benjamin, as each of them had personally experienced this cruel wisdom—Benjamin looking at you, and remembering the day you were born, and knowing what day you were in, and foreseeing the day you would die. And then, Benjamin turning coolly away, and rather than weeping, saying—

"Hard life goes on," which was the other thing he said.

But tonight, as Benjamin lifted his head to look out at the figures crossing the hayfield, an animation, however briefly, flitted across his face. In his expression, there was fear, and glee—and even hope. All the animals were riveted on Benjamin—*what would he make of the figures?* Even the three steeds—who were argued by the sheep to be the dumbest animals on the farm—knew enough to gauge Benjamin for some answer.

The cows lowed—

"What is it? What do you remember, Benjamin?"

Benjamin, having known many of the cows for a long time, would, on rare occasion, help them to remember. But tonight, as rare an occasion as it might be, he just backed away from the missing slat, and gave no answer.

Startlingly—so much closer than the barking at the gate, the animals heard the bloodcurdling growl of dogs. Just outside the barn doors, two of the German shepherds had borne down upon the strangers. The canine rumble was as horrifying as an opened vein, and the animals cowered, as if to hide their own blood.

And yet, the pig answered the menace in a voice confident and knowing—

"I have seen larger dogs than you. I have smelled them. They are pungent with bear and cougar. They would take you in their jaws and carry you to their burrows, where they would feed you to their young. I have made these dogs my dogs. And now you will be my dogs—or you will be meat and bone."

The pair of dogs, so fierce only a moment before, tested their voices to bark, and heard emanate from their own throats no more than pathetic yelps.

"Sit," said the pig. And the two dogs sat.

The cows, who didn't much like the dogs, as they were an aggressive lot who were always getting underhoof, recognized an eminence in this pig, and they directed the cat—

"Unlatch the barn door."

Norma, scuttling down the rail to the hayloft, pawed, pawed, at the wooden lever, until the door swung wide—and the finely tailored pig crossed the threshold into the dim kerosene glow of the barn.

Upon sight of the animal, there was the hoarse craw of the raven, Moses, who, high above in the rafters, none of the animals had known was in attendance—

"Snowball!"

The two guard dogs, at the sound of the name, managed to overcome their fear—and growled again as they rose from their haunches. But with merely a twist of the head, the pig turned them back. They shrank and whimpered—

"I'm a small dog. Small."

The raven crawed again—

"It's Snowball!"

The name, to many of the animals, did not have the resonance that one might expect, as their memories were too short. But after a minute or so of murmuring, most of those present had an inkling of who Snowball was—and his wicked lot in history.

The cows definitely remembered that, however many years ago, Snowball had snuck in during the days to upset the pails, and in the nights, to milk them in their sleep. The chickens also retained some idea of Snowball—breaking eggs and stealing corn. And even a few of the sheep thought they remembered that Snowball had destroyed the windmill.

Snowball held out his hooves—

"You have been told that I trampled the spring shoots. That I gnawed the bark off fruit trees. That I broke windows and blocked drains. That I stole the key to the store shed and threw it down the well. That I planted weeds, and mixed their seed with the seed of the vegetables. That I conspired with the enemy farms of Foxwood and Pinchfield!"

The animals broke into a wild tumult. They clacked and snorted to each other in anger—yes, they had heard of the traitor Snowball! The villain, Snowball!

Raising his voice above the din, Snowball continued—

"You have heard that I am a spreader of lies and rumors. That I was an agent of evil from the very start. But I ask you now to remember, not what you have heard, but what you have seen!"

And with that, Snowball stripped himself of his blazer, his tie, his cufflinks, and his shirt. This was not the chest of any pig that any of the animals had seen in a long, long time. Few remembered having ever seen an old pig so muscular and lean. Where the pigs of the farm were fat and decrepit, Snowball had a body that every animal in the barn recognized as his own body—hard with years of hard sorrow and hard work.

The Yorkshire boar turned, and showed the scars on his pink back—buckshot. Wicked burns striped his flesh. And the animals, now gathering together into the center of the barn, began to talk amongst themselves. Someone remembered that Snowball had attempted to have them all killed at the Battle of Windmill. No, someone else remembered, it was the Battle of Cowshed—and he was only censured for cowardice. One of the brighter cows seemed to recollect that it was Napoleon who had inflicted the wound upon Snowball—but that was with his teeth, not buckshot.

Their eyes questioning, the animals turned to Benjamin, as he was the sole creature who remembered things exactly the way they happened. But Benjamin wasn't revealing anything.

"Life's always hard," he said, in his usual cryptic manner.

"I swear to you," Snowball interjected, in a tremulous voice hard to disbelieve, "that I received these wounds ready to give my life—to die—for Animal Farm."

Here, all gasped. Nobody uttered those banned words in public. Sometimes the words were heard in private conversations, or in silent prayers to some distant, glimmering future—but never in public. The shepherds would surely devour him.

But, they didn't.

Snowball was alive.

"It's, it's called the Manor Farm," squeaked a nervous rat.

"No," said Snowball with total resolve—

"It is called Animal Farm!"

There was another gasp, then silence. Then the raven Moses croaked from the rafters—

"Where have you come from, Snowball? Have you returned from Sugarcandy Mountain?"

Few could fathom why the cawing of this common raven was tolerated by the pigs. Moses was always sitting around on some perch somewhere, decrying the virtues of the age-old myth of Sugarcandy Mountain—a place, he said, just above the clouds, where it was Sunday everyday, and clover was always in season, and lump sugar and linseed cake flowered from bushes. More often than not, he would be drinking from the gill of beer that he was officially allotted each day by the pigs. (For only a quarter-pint, he seemed to drink quite often, and quite heartily.) But Moses, despite his porcine sponsorship, wasn't much listened to by the animals. His audience was generally filled out by the few Sugarcandy zealots—mostly troubled, troubling souls, who were themselves better left ignored. Perhaps, it had now and again been suggested, Moses was kept on tap for the simple reason that he diverted those maniacs from making real trouble.

At any rate, to the vast majority of the farm animals, Moses had been telling his tales of Sugarcandy Mountain for far too long, with, aside from his beer quota, far too little result.

"Really," Moses breathlessly repeated—

"Aren't you back from Sugarcandy Mountain?"

Moses made his suggestion with a kind of hypnotic sway. But far from inspiring awe, the bird elicited no more than a single snort (one of the steers), which was followed by a collective caterwaul and boo. *What an annoyance that Moses should insist on voicing this absurdity!* Even Snowball hardly grunted a dismissal. The question, apparently, was too far beneath his dignity to address at all.

Still bare-chested, the lean pig lifted his hooves as high as they would go.

"It is true that I have been far away."

"But Snowball," asked a sad-eyed lamb with ears and a muzzle of deep brown, "where have you been?"

And Snowball replied—

"I have been on a dangerous mission—in the village."

Animals gulped with fear. Animals *oohh-ed*, animals *aahh-ed*. Snowball continued triumphantly.

"But now—still alive!—I return to you, old Matilda the cow, and you, old Frido the sheep," and here, Snowball paused to look deeply into the eyes of the two elderly animals, who didn't seem to have the faintest memory of ever having seen him before, "For so long have I missed you, my dear old friends. And so too, as absence makes the heart grow fonder, am I swelling with a love for each and every one of you!"

The well-dressed goat pawed Snowball a handkerchief. Snowball dabbed at his eye.

"And with this pride in my chest, I do bring to you—a better way!"

One of the younger lambs repeated, "a better way, a better way," and Snowball only just silenced him before the other sheep joined in and the meeting was overwhelmed by their chanting.

"I have searched from the hillcrest to the vale," Snowball nodded his head gravely, "And tonight, I present an animalage of such erudition that all the wisdom of the village is now ours." Snowball turned to the genteel goat behind him. The goat, his fine silver hair elegantly coifed, bowed with his hoof at the trim waist of his pinstriped suit—a blend of silk and tropical wool.

And it was then that any forward momentum was lost—as with the scratch of three-toed feet, and a flutter of down, the last of the avian population, having finally gathered in such mass as to push open the door, flocked into the barn. There were the geese and ducks from the pond, the hens from the henhouse, the roosters from the rooster coop, and the pigeons from the pigeon coop. And thus assembled, the winged audience grew bold—voiced its confusion. Not known to be particularly intelligent, the ruffled latecomers proved exceedingly difficult to unruffle. The meeting sputtered to a standstill, as Snowball was forced to repeat, and reiterate previous minutes. When Snowball came to the part about a better way, the sheep could not contain themselves, and broke out into a mantra of "a better way," which lasted for five minutes.

It was not until the black cockerel was heard a-cock-a-doodle-dooing that the Shropshires finally hushed. The doodle-doo of that cockerel was a harbinger to heed with terror, as it could mean only one thing—

"Minimus is coming," whispered Norma the cat.

Minimus, like the leaders who'd preceded him, was always led by a heraldic black cockerel, who served as a kind of trumpeter. Upon entering the barn, the cockerel, still doodle-dooing, was immediately followed by a pack of dogs—the most vicious on the farm. These were Minimus's personal guard. Directly into the barnhouse marched the procession—and behind them, marched Minimus himself.

In spite of the similarities, Minimus, unlike his predecessors, left a distinct impression that he wasn't too happy with it all. Yes, like the others, he did wear a whip. But unlike Squealer or Napoleon, he never used it, and had been overheard saying he didn't much like the damnable thing and only carried it because all the other pigs carried them—and he didn't feel like going around, amongst a lot like that, the only one without a whip.

Minimus was an old fat pig with a scholarly disposition. Always in his smoking jacket, he gave off an exceedingly literary, if conservative air. The fact of the matter was that

Minimus didn't really enjoy running the show—he'd rather be reading Shakespeare.

Minimus's dogs, however, were not so indifferent. Nor were they so easily frightened as had been those dogs at the barn door. All the animals were aware, these dogs would attack if Minimus gave the order. Their commander, Minimus's Top Dog, was an all-gray brute named, aptly, Brutus. It was known around that Brutus would not back down—that he was not scared of anything. Once, he had taken on a den of snakes. Nevertheless, Brutus, being a dog who believed profoundly in the chain of command, prided himself on an absolute loyalty. So, when Minimus raised his thick snout and uttered, "Stay," Brutus, with his soldiers, stayed.

The dogs under Brutus's command had an instinctual hatred of Snowball. To them, he was simply an outsider—at the time of Snowball's departure, few of these shepherds had even been born, and not a one remembered him, or his hog's smell. Grimly, they grrrr-ed. Dogs didn't like change.

Brutus snarled at the upstart—

"So you tell them you're Snowball—and they believe you. That doesn't make it so."

This, agreed the animals, was a point that warranted some serious consideration. After all, even if they presently believed it was Snowball, why should they continue to believe it was Snowball? Why, without any evidence to the contrary, they could easily change their minds, and decide it wasn't Snowball.

Minimus, his jowls shaking as he vigorously nodded his head in agreement, redoubled the argument of his Top Dog—

"And even if you are Snowball, just because you say Snowball wasn't bad, that doesn't make that so, either."

And this, again, was a point well taken. Logically—and it made two of the sheep pass out to have it all in their heads—

whether or not this pig was Snowball, Snowball might have been no good.

"You," Minimus contemptuously deduced, "might be an imposter and a liar."

The duplicity of this—the highly sophisticated level of deception that was suggested—made another one of the sheep pass out. And two of the geese needed to step out of the barn for air. And yet, as much as everyone longed for clarity, Minimus, having cocked his head to one side, was still making up his mind—as to who and what this pig and his goat represented.

Norma the cat was the first to realize the only way this issue might be incontrovertibly resolved—

"You have to tell us, Benjamin."

And Benjamin the donkey lifted his head to a whole barn that awaited the truth. Even Minimus, overwhelmed by circumstance, had turned to the donkey to remember. . . .

Benjamin scanned the animals of the Manor Farm. The geese, the ganders, the goslings, the ewes, the rams, the lambs, the mares, the steeds, the foals . . . and the pigs.

Benjamin looked behind Minimus to the entourage of swine, mostly Tamworths, that was now arriving. Following on their heels, German shepherds briefed their masters in veiled voices.

Minimus's brown sow wore a red skirt suit. (It had taken her so long to change that it seemed to confirm the rumor of her preference for French lingerie after 8 PM, and subsequent to that hour, her pronounced reluctance to wear anything else.) Higgledy-piggledy, she and all the porkers were waddling in— pizza hanging from their snouts, cookie dough in their hooves.

"You have mustard on your shirt," said one pig to another.

"Oh," said the first, licking up the dollop of mustard, "why, thank you."

With their black eyes, the animals beseeched the donkey to give them the answer—

Was it Snowball? Could a pig be their friend? What was the truth?

But Benjamin shook his head, no. No, he didn't care anymore. No, he didn't see any reason to distinguish one pig from another.

No.

Withdrawing into his stall, Benjamin closed his eyes and lifted up one leg. He was a bit deaf, and would have no trouble going back to sleep. . . .

Minimus exhaled wheezily.

It was up to him.

He knew it would be. Everything petty and meaningless was up to him. *Was this Snowball? And if so, who was Snowball? A traitor or a hero?* Minimus looked into the eyes, and the heart, of the pig before him. And then, Minimus looked into his own heart.

Always a bit of a softie, Minimus, in his old age, had gone softer. Not to undervalue his considerable achievements—it was now Minimus who was Leader—who inhabited his own apartment in the Jones House—who had two dogs to wait upon him—who ate off the Crown Derby dinner service— who drank his daily half-gallon of beer from the soup tureen. And yet, where Minimus was very much like the other pigs, in that he was soft on the outside, he was not like them, in that he was soft on the inside. The other pigs would chew out the heart of an enemy were their nightly beer threatened—but Minimus didn't really care about stuff like that. All the milk and apples left him empty. He had always suspected he had a soul so pure as a dove's, and he suffered a salient regret, a remorse, that he had not been stronger, that he had not been greater, that he had not shown the fortitude to be faithful to himself—to be kinder, gentler to his own ideals . . . and, maybe, to the farm.

Snowball (or the Yorkshire making a mighty lot of claims about Snowball) broke the silence—

"Do you know the old pigpen?" he asked Matilda the cow, who nodded yes. "Bed it with hay, for me and my associate. We will sleep nowhere else."

The old cow, not sure what to do with this questionable order from this questionable source, shuffled anxiously, and mooed to the pig she was certain was her Leader—Minimus. And Minimus, that Berkshire boar as fat and handsome and chocolate black as any a Berkshire boar that ever walked on two hooves, made his decision. Tears welled up in his eyes, for however insignificant this decision might turn out to be, he understood somehow that with it he was striving towards that magnanimity that would raise him up to history.

His weighty throat resonant with emotion, Minimus spoke—

"Cow, get him his bedding, and make him comfortable—and make him welcome. He is Snowball, Animal Hero, First Class, of the Battle of Cowshed."

II

IT WAS MADE KNOWN during the week that the Sunday Meeting was to resume. For years, after the Sunday morning raising of the green flag, the "Meeting" had taken the form of a general assembly, where any animal might voice an opinion to the powers that be. (The pigs.) The Meeting had been cancelled under the leadership of Napoleon, as it had been decided the whole thing was really just too much trouble, and rather tiring besides. The assembly had been replaced by marching and parading, which, though rousing at first, had itself become a drudge that was eventually phased out. Only at the occasional sporting festival (a day of races, and contests of strength, eating, and drinking) was everyone forced to wave that familiar green flag, and chant—

"Manor Farm forever, I pledge my meat and leather."

With considerable apprehension, the reinstated Sunday Meeting was anticipated—as there was consensus among those not-pig that nothing good had ever happened at the Meeting, though all agreed, without exception, that as a whole everything was much better than it used to be. Why, they once were much hungrier. (And when was that? In the days before the rebellion, or after? Well, all good things came from suffering, as the pigs always said with a guttural chuckle.)

It was known that private conferences between Snowball

and Minimus were underway, and that these would largely decide the agenda and tenor of the Sunday Meeting. As the week wore on, the cheerful countenances of Snowball, Minimus, and the majority of the pigs left most of the animals feeling a sort of tenuous optimism. It seemed as if whatever was in the works wasn't all that threatening—and the pigs, especially Snowball, were disposed to an unusual friendliness. On Thursday, each animal received one spoonful of applesauce. Snowball even helped (with his own hooves!) in tending the hayfield, the vegetable patches, and the grain. Though it was too early yet to know for sure, he said the crop seemed in good order—and he complimented every animal, at whatever task, on the fine work that he or she had accomplished.

"We couldn't do it without you," he would say.

And, remarkably, this little encouragement from such an important pigage made an empty manger seem less of an obstacle on a long afternoon. "Lunch" was but a faded memory to most of the farm animals, and when Snowball spoke of having it too reinstated, even the overseers, who, being pigs, had never themselves rescinded the pastime, were swept up in the dizzifying good humor, and let out a few vicarious yips of joy for their elated workers.

One pig who did not share in this sunny disposition was Pinkeye. Pinkeye was the pig the most old school of the new school. And as he trailed behind Minimus in Minimus's retinue, one could see that whatever they were to be, the reforms had left him looking like he'd eaten an old lemon. Despite talk, early in the week, that Snowball would assume Pinkeye's position of Next Leader, the tenure had gone unthreatened—as Snowball avowed an absolute disinterest in officialdom. Nevertheless, as the week wore on, Pinkeye's expression grew so exceptionally dour that it made an animal wince and turn away. That was no expression to be seen on the face of a pig with a whip! Years ago, Pinkeye had served as Napoleon's food taster, and the cows, who had some memory of this, joked that maybe something didn't taste entirely right. . . .

Interestingly, however, Pinkeye seemed to be getting on famously with Snowball, who was teaching him to do something called "croquet." A box of the supplies necessary for this diversion had been delivered from downtown Willingdon, and a field was cleared from the weeds behind the Jones House that the two white boars might engage themselves in the mysterious and probably important activity.

Finally, Sunday morning came—and after a treat of dried figs, the (new) old Sunday Morning meeting was called to order with the hoisting of the Manor Farm green flag. All the animals of the farm were in attendance. Cows, sheep, goats, horses, rats, cats, ducks, pigeons, geese, chickens, raven, and, standing with Minimus along the back wall, that disquieting retinue of black cockerels, dogs, boars, and heavily made-up sows.

From the elevation of an overturned wash-bin (placed several feet frontward of the back wall) Snowball addressed the entire barn. "Ahhh," Pinkeye was heard to whisper, "an orator of the days of yore."

But Snowball, having only just lifted his foreleg to clear his throat into his hoof, found his place of esteem declining—as the wash-bin was wrinkling beneath his very trotters. In only a moment, he stood atop what looked to be a crumpled birthday cake.

"Aha," said Snowball, "well perhaps we might amend the situation . . . with this!"

Having heard their cue, two bulls suddenly banged through the barn doors. Before them, they pushed a monstrous construction of marble, granite, and chrome.

Shortly, the bulls had positioned the goliath, and Snowball, having mounted it, explained—

"Now this is a proper soapbox."

Indeed, most of the animals had heard something about speaking from a soapbox—and if that's what a soapbox was, well, without question, it far exceeded any turned up wash-bin. To stand nestled in that cradle of shining stone was definitely attention getting.

No doubt about it—quite authoritative.

Without a word, Snowball waved his hoof as if to say, *a gift, think nothing of it,* and the barn let out a hurrah of approval for the bedazzling marble thing—and then the meeting was underway.

"Your Leader, Minimus," said Snowball, and here, he paused to allow Minimus the Leader to eyeball the ensemble, "has set forth his goal—a total overhaul of our way of life! And better days, every day, for every one of you!"

The sheep burst out into "Better day, every day," and only quieted after several long minutes.

"But first, we must decide—who shall lead us in this quest? Will it be Minimus, who himself has envisioned this new and better day? Will it be Minimus, who is what you might call 'pigheaded' in his absolute determination to guide us to this new and better day?"

"Minimus! Minimus! Yes! Yes! Better day! Better day!" enjoined the sheep.

Snowball continued on the subject of a new leadership position titled, "Prize Pig," and a new method of choosing the leader, called election. After a brief explanation as to what a candidate was, Minimus took a moment on the soapbox to read a brief statement which Snowball passed off to him. The barn animals seemed to like it, then Minimus got back down, and Snowball resumed his place—

"We call for a vote! Vote Minimus for Prize Pig!"

Ballots were distributed. The animals were instructed that they were free to vote as they wished, and on how to scratch out the single perforated box without leaving a hanging chad. The ballots were collected and tallied. Then the results were in—a landslide! Minimus, nodding smugly, read another prepared statement, congratulated Pinkeye, who would assume the role of Next Prize Pig, then ceded the soapbox to Snowball.

And Snowball—he raised his hooves high.

Almost as high as his ears!

"Minimus thanks you for your support—and for this opportunity to make a difference for all of us! What he proposes now is nothing short of a new rebellion. And in that rebellion, we shall follow our Prize Pig, Minimus, to victory!"

Minimus, behind Snowball, was still nodding—his double chins still shaking.

"First on Minimus's agenda—our illustrious anthem shall be returned to its place of honor in our hearts! So let us now sing *Beasts of Earth*."

At this, the animals shifted uncomfortably on their hocks, for while most had heard that there was once an anthem of some kind, none knew it. Fortunately, Snowball had taken the appropriate steps, and pages with the printed lyrics were distributed. The animals who couldn't read too well were helped by those who could. Only Benjamin looked at the words with a leery eye—always suspicious, that old donkey.

Led by the pigs and dogs, who had evidently reviewed the anthem, the animals began to sing—

> *Beasts of Earth, it is our fate*
> *To live in one gigantic state*
> *Of happy days and cool, sweet grapes.*

We know not what the struggle brings
But we are bonded, loyal friends,
Of freedom carried on the wind.

Beasts of Earth, now unite
And fight the happy, happy fight.
For freedom is a laughing riot.

Ha ha, ho ho, hear us chuckle.
Beasts of Earth come join the bustle—
And learn to dance The Freedom Shuffle!

And with that, Snowball and Minimus, and all the pigs and dogs (even Brutus and Pinkeye!) began a kind of side-step dance routine. And the animals, many of whom were not too swift at mental-type things, were quickly able to imitate the move—as, much more so than humans, animals tend to be rather adept physically. It didn't take long before every one of them, down to the three horses who could only recite the alphabet to the letter B, had practically mastered The Freedom Shuffle. (So this was what Snowball had learned out there in the village!) It was a catchy thing to the feet, and before they knew it, the animals found themselves singing the (new) old anthem, *Beasts of Earth*, while at the same time executing the maneuver. And after the first time, they did it four more times. The animals, even the pigs and dogs, reveled in the song—not only in the group dancing, which was a new experience for all, but to have their voices joined together once again.

Just like the days of the rebellion!

And the thing so nice about it, was that now, with no more than a little song and side-step, they could feel like this whenever they wanted—even when they were working in the fields!

It was then announced by Snowball, that by the Prize Pig's decree, the Manor Farm would henceforth be known by its proper name—

Animal Farm.

The sheep chanted it for the rest of the afternoon—

"Animal Farm."

It was only a few days before all the animals were old pros at The Freedom Shuffle—and a near-on continual singing and humming and re-remembering of that long forgotten song, *Beasts of Earth*, had almost entirely supplanted the ditty which had, all those years ago, replaced it. (*Animal Farm, Animal Farm. /Never through me shall thou come to harm!*) Though Minimus had been the author of this secondary trill, he didn't seem to much mind the purge. One would almost think, in fact, from the pleasure Minimus exhibited in hearing the (new) old anthem, that he had penned it himself.

The next Sunday Meeting, after the singing of the song, *Beasts of Earth*, the green flag, which had been run up the flag-pole to call the assembly, was taken down. And in the witness of the entire snorting, barking, and chirruping assembly, an updated flag was raised. Still green, this flag was painted with an orange hoof, a purple horn, and a yellow wing. Though the design was utterly new and exciting to all, it had, inexplicably, a faintly familiar feel which put everyone at ease.

"This flag represents our boundless faith in Animal Farm," explained Snowball—

"The green represents the enormous bounty that the farm offers—fields of clover for everyone! And the hoof, horn, and wing represent all the animals who can have, if they work together, this future of wonderment! It doesn't matter if you're purple, yellow, or orange—this farm is your farm!"

As one might expect, there was an outcry of joy—especially

about the clover. Fields of clover for all of us, the cows whispered to each other, greatly impressed.

Following the raising of the new flag, the animals proceeded to the back of the barnhouse, where more changes had been put in place for them. Most of the animals side-stepped, though they had not been strictly instructed to do so.

Here, there were several gulps and exclamations. ("Welladay!" and "Gracious to goodness!" said the geese.) And, as was becoming a regular occurrence in these surprising times, two of the sheep fainted.

The bronze statue of Napoleon, which for the longest of times had replaced the skull of Old Major, was no place to be seen.

"Wh-wh-where," stuttered the frightened animals, "is the protector of the sheepfold, the duckling's friend, the godfather of geese?"

"Friends," said Snowball, "it is true that Napoleon was a great Leader." Snowball turned to the pigs, "It is true that he was the paradigm of pigs." Snowball turned to the dogs, "It is true that he was the terror of mankind." And here, Snowball turned to all, "But it is also true that his foremost commitment was that nothing should get in the way of your living the goodest, fullest lives."

"Goodest, fullest lives," repeated the sheep.

"And yes," said Snowball, "now is a time when our lives can be gooder, and fuller. Napoleon's time, that's the past—while now is a time for the future. And we must not hesitate—for Napoleon would not hesitate. No, Napoleon would not hesitate to sacrifice anything—to give you that gooderest, fullerest life. No, Napoleon would not even hesitate—to sacrifice himself!"

"No, not even himself," mewled Norma ecstatically, carried away by the moment.

"Well," concurred Snowball, casting Norma a sympathetic

eye, "I too will sacrifice anything for you, as would Minimus or Pinkeye or Brutus—just because we love you. Anything—for your own good."

At this, there was a cheer. "For our own good, for own good," repeated the sheep.

And just like that, Napoleon and his days were pretty well forgotten—and that, perhaps, was the objective. What's more, in days to come, it would often altogether slip an animal's mind that he or she was led by anyone. It would seem, ever increasingly, that what he or she did was by his or her own design.

With the broad sweep of a white muslin sheet pulled away from the side of the barn, Snowball pointed dramatically to the new Commandment—

All animals are born equal—what they become is their own affair.

Yes, yes, all nodded their heads with collective assurance—that seemed fair enough. What we become is our own affair, each of them thought, confident that on a level playing field they could be enormously successful. So . . . fair enough! The pigs nodded. The dogs nodded. And all of the animals nodded. Why, it was a miracle! Except for old Benjamin, who wasn't nodding, it seemed that everyone, truly, was in complete accord!

Yes, yes, yes, yes, yes—it was entirely obvious that Snowball really had learned a great deal out there in the village!

To conclude the Meeting, it was additionally revealed that the old portrait of Napoleon had been replaced—this time with the image of some hard-working horse named Boxer, whom nobody but the pigs, and presumably, Benjamin remembered. It certainly was a moving depiction, however, and several noticed that Benjamin was not just teary-eyed, but positively sobbing at the sight of it. In the rendering, the brave horse pulled a cart of stone up an endless slope. . . .

In an unscheduled issuance, Snowball had the dogs tear down a final white sheet, to reveal an ode to Animal Farm that he had written to replace the now obsolete, *Founding Father Napoleon*. The ode was called, *All Animals Eat Pie*.

You may disagree on a bed or a sty.
You may be annoyed when your food's full of flies.
But never ask, "why's that manger better than mine?"
'Cause they worked really hard, and we all like pie.

The change was a surprise to all. ("Halloo!" cried the sheep.) And even Minimus, the author of the original poem, *Founding Father Napoleon*, seemed caught off guard. At first, the Prize Pig appeared to prickle, and pucker—but then he had on his face something sort of resembling approval (albeit a twisted and tense approval). After all, it was a premise hard to refute—everyone did like pie.

At the next Sunday Meeting, Snowball presented Minimus's "architecture for a better future." He explained that out there in the village, one learned that there was nothing wrong with humans—and there was nothing wrong with living with them, or like them. To be perfectly frank, stated Snowball, in a village full of humans, it was probably "a good idea" to live with them, and like them. And when an animal heard it said that the prosperity of the one was the prosperity of the other—well, it could sometimes be a lie, but it could also be the truth. Because really, when one thought about it, the prosperity of animals was the prosperity of men, and the prosperity of men was the prosperity of animals. As long as the two lived together in the same village—their fortunes were utterly dependent on one another. And one might as well face up to it. Men and animals together in Willingdon. Yes, perhaps in competition, but also in fraternity.

Basic instruction in walking on two legs and wearing clothes would commence first thing Monday morning, said Snowball. And the animals supposed that, probably, there wasn't anything wrong with walking on two legs or wearing clothes. They had all seen the pigs walking and wearing clothes for years. It just looked like it might put a little strain on the lower back, and be a little cramped—that was all.

For many years, said Snowball, sharing his history, he had been a student of the goat by his side, whom he called Thomas, as well as something broader, which he called "the village out there." He had seen something called "economy," and having analyzed this systematization of resources, he had arrived, with Thomas's help, at a plan to revitalize the farm. And at this juncture he hesitated, suggesting that perhaps now it would be better to let Thomas himself take over. And Snowball preceded his yielding of the animal audience by introducing Thomas the goat as the most educated animal he had ever met, or even heard of. Upon him, this goat had had conferred the degrees of Doctor, Lawyer, Architect, and Engineer.

Taking his place on the soapbox, Thomas addressed the barnhouse. His elocution was so very sophisticated and genteel that many of the animals—dumbstruck—suddenly forgot to close their mouths, snouts, or beaks. Nobody had ever heard an animal talk like that.

"Dear me, thoroughly an honor to be so introduced by my esteemed colleague, Snowball, Animal Hero First Class. To address this issue of 'betterness,' inclusive of tomorrow and tomorrow's tomorrow, and naturally, inclusive of all of you, and tomorrow's all of you, I can, I am perfectly positive — and I say this without qualification, hesitation, or prevarication — provide the manner of your deliverance. I propose to you an electrical generator, which will light your stalls, warm your stalls, cool your stalls, plough your fields, seed your fields, reap/bind/sort your crops, milk your udders, knead your bread, and slice your turnips."

There were gasps from all corners — this seemed too good to be possible.

"Also," the goat drawled, "I assure you that I will furnish every stall with hot and cold water!"

Four sheep fell on their sides — two cooperative steers dragged them outside for a breath of fresh air.

"But how?" asked Norma for the entire barn.

To answer, Snowball thanked Thomas and resumed his place on the soapbox —

"Windmills. Two of them. And these will not only be much easier to build than the one we already have — they'll run much more efficiently. With the help of Thomas, Doctor, Architect, Engineer, and Lawyer, we'll be finished in two months time." (Another sheep passed out.) And the following morning, while the animals attended their first classes on walking and wearing clothes, Thomas and the pigs began to draft the plans for the Twin Mills.

III

MOSES THE RAVEN did not miss a single Sunday Meeting—though none of the animals could tell when Moses might come or go throughout the rest of the week, or where he spent his nights on those nights he did not remain on the farm. Nor did any of the other animals know that following every Sunday Meeting, Moses flew over the hayfield, over the orchard, over the pond, and came to the arch of the stream, far beyond the reach of the pigs—and from there, crossed into the Woodlands, to the encampment of the beavers.

Animal Farm was sandwiched between Foxwood Farm, to the west, and Pinchfield Farm, to the east. To the north lay the road—to the south, the Woodlands. The borders of the three farms extended well into the Woodlands—to the top of a rocky undulation of forest that was too big to call a hill, and too small to call a mountain. A stream, as it ran down the slope of the uncultivatable land, looped through Foxwood, Animal Farm, and Pinchfield—and then, as it reached plowed ground, swung back, this time through Pinchfield, Animal Farm, and Foxwood. By this common water source, the three farms were forever embraced—the one unriskable betrayal, an interruption of the water supply. As each farm owned its individual up-river portion of the Woodlands, should any one farm cut off water to any other, that cut-off farm would immediately retaliate by cutting off the water source of the aggressor. The final outcome of such a conflict being a triad of dry fields, the farms always managed to cooperate on the matter of the stream. This cooperative even went so far as to jointly monitor the all-important flow down the useless Woodlands hump.

Aside from a bit of trapping on the part of Pinchfield and Foxwood, the only benefit the Woodlands seemed to offer was the satisfaction won from occasionally clearing a beaver dam with a bit of dynamite. This was a small matter to the farms, attended with the casual stick—and outside the gratified guffaw of a job well done, nobody gave it much thought. On Animal Farm, few outside the pigs were even aware of the operations. The sporadic kablooeys spooked the horses—but they were calmed once it was explained that the brook had just been cleared of an obstruction, and that the water in their troughs would be colder and fresher in a matter of no time at all.

The beavers, however, to whom Moses returned after the Sunday Meetings, were not nearly so blithe about the destruction of their dams. The leader of the beavers—who had come to power with the promise that he would return control of the water supply to the beaver paw, where it belonged—was Diso. Forced from their lodges (where, under the threat of dynamite, only the most immobile and helpless creatures dared continued habitation) Diso and his troops were bunkered deep underground—in dens built by field squirrels, moles, and rabbits.

As difficult as it was in the Woodlands to just scrape by without having to do anything extra, those field squirrels, moles, and rabbits hadn't much appreciated the extensive excavating required to develop the beaver burrows. And yet, when the order to dig had been given down, it had been followed, as the more militant beavers commanded a total dominion in the Woodlands. The Woodlands animals, who had been hunted and trapped for so long, thirsted for a leadership that could satiate their anger, and perhaps even reckon with the evils of "farmland." It might be true, they all agreed, that the beavers were possibly a little too forceful—but to the spring-traps of the previous season, the deer had lost four doe, a buck, and two fawns, and the rabbits had lost twenty, and the ducks had lost four, and the voles had lost seven, and the pheasants had lost five, and the squirrels had lost six, and the mice had lost two, and the moles had lost one. And the newts, frogs, and toads had lost forty-seven to that evil incarnate, Bilby Pilkington, son to the owner of the Foxwood farm—a boy of eleven with a penchant for arming his slingshot with live amphibians. The Woodlands animals needed protection, and if the beavers were a little too fervent, a little too excitable, well, it was just the way the cricket crunched.

"What have you for me?" Diso lifted his head from heavy books and worn blueprints when the raven crept into the candlelit den—

"What word do you deliver, my herald Moses?"

Much unlike his status on Animal Farm, in the Woodlands (where Animal Farm was more commonly known as the "Pig Farm"), the raven Moses had been raised to a status of semi-divinity. Once Moses had explained to the newly empowered beavers that ravens lived for 300 years, and that he himself was 200 and therefore remembered the greatness of long-ago days when beavers ruled the village—well then, the beavers bestowed upon Moses a state of holy grace. A state, to Moses, of the most exquisite bliss. A state, moreover, of that rarest optimism—perhaps, he thought, if the beavers really were to control the village, he would always receive this lauding, which he so rightly, and obviously, obviously, obviously, deserved. And in return for this ecstasy, Moses had imparted to the beavers the old knowledge (from the Age of Beavers) as he himself remembered it. The herald had restored to the beavers the tenets of the Ancient Beaver Code, which disallowed, specifically, any indulging in lemon meringue pies, and, more generally, any indulging in pies, period. So, as a matter of course, Diso was intensely concerned when Moses reported the new Pig Farm credo, "We all like pie," as it was undoubtedly a threat to the Ancient Beaver Code, if not, indeed, a direct assault on it.

Diso was a firm believer in the Ancient Beaver Code, and he followed it dutifully. He brushed his body fur to the left, and his tail fur to the right, four times a day—as did the followers of the Ancient Beaver Code from the time when beavers ruled the village and all was good. Also, as was the way of the pure European beaver (and Diso himself was a fine specimen of that rare genus, *Castor fiber*), he always walked on four legs—as did every other animal in the Woodlands. Only the birds walked on two legs, and there had been some discussion of requiring them—if they were absolutely determined to insist on walking—to drag their wingtips as they did so.

For the beavers, whose minds had been so yearning for this historical perspective now offered by Moses, it was almost inconceivable that back on the"Piggery" their herald raven was considered at best a clown or a liar, and at worst, a bore. The beavers couldn't understand that the animals on the Pig Farm had just, over the years, tired of the over-familiar raven, and grown to distrust him. Not to say the farm animals wouldn't have liked a new raven, if one arrived—they held no grudges against any species. It was just Moses they were sick of. But from the perspective of the beavers, this thinly veiled antagonism to Moses, an invaluable source of spiritual wisdom and deeper understanding, meant only one thing—the animals on the farm were nincompoops.

Diso was no nincompoop. As a young beaver, he had left the woods to seek out the education of the village goats. And only when Diso had learned all he could from the Swiss Toggenburgs did he return to the Woodlands. Diso had been well trained in the history not only of his own land—but in the histories of the land that surrounded him. He knew all about Foxwood—a farm owned by Mr. Pilkington, a cavalier gentleman farmer who liked killing deer and carp. And he knew all about Pinchfield, which was owned by a Mr. Frederick, a cunning devil who reveled in filing lawsuits, and beating every last penny out of his land and livestock. And Diso, as well, knew all about the Pig Farm—about the endless avarice and deceit of the swine, and the ruthless way that they, like the humans, bombed the beaver dams. More than anything else, Diso knew about that hypocrisy—and those lying hogs. They treated animals no better than humans treated animals, and therefore, were no better than humans. Most of the Woodlands didn't even understand that there had been a rebellion on the Pig Farm. The Woodlands animals had hated their mistreatment back when the Pig Farm was the Manor Farm, owned by Mr. Jones. And they hated their mistreatment now, when it was owned by the pigs. It was all the same to them. And as much as the militant Diso was feared and even resented by much of the Woodlands population, there was still that incontrovertible thing—waterflow was their right.

As of late, the intelligence that Diso had collected on the Pig Farm was particularly comprehensive. Moses, who regularly reported to Diso on all three of the nincompoop farms, had been explicit in his account of the recent changes that were now taking place on the Pig Farm—under the dictate of the pig Minimus, and more importantly, the pig Snowball.

Also, there were the rats, who, always back and forth between the Woodlands and the three farms (based upon wherever life was easiest at the moment), could be relied upon for the most up-to-date news. Rats, though they had nearly no long-term memories, had excellent short-term memories— virtually photographic. And thus, they made exceptional spies and saboteurs—as they could be told anything about the past, and they would believe it, and they would do anything for you, and then forget it. The only problem with rats was that they were so greedy for chicken eggs, peanut butter, and coconut strips smeared with limburger, that they wouldn't stop at making things up or exaggerating their tales to increase a dividend.

But despite the weaknesses of the sources—from the greed of the rats to the vagueness of Moses, who, though highly esteemed, was not known for his directness—the beavers, by their extremely technical minds, felt they could sort it all out. The beaver brain, suited to a task so complex as to go beyond the wildest arrogant imaginings of any other animal (that task being dam building), was uniquely adapted to sifting variant information into a cosmological entirety—an entirety that went all the way back to that time only Moses remembered, when beavers oversaw a village in harmony with the universe. . . .

"Up there," Moses would point into the night sky—

"Up there you see the Lodestar of Sugarcandy, where, for every righteous beaver, 1600 virgin birch saplings await."

And accordingly, being the chosen population of the Lodestar, and having for years had both Moses and their diverse intelligence operations, the beavers supposed that they had a pretty good grasp of things—one that was getting better every day. (At that time of earthly departure, this ongoing striving for clarity would surely, and promptly so, plop a soul on the Lodestar.) And with the new information that had been provided by Moses, the Pig Farm, to the beaver's way of thinking, was not only the most reprehensible of the Woodlands enemies, but also the most well understood.

The hypocrite pig!

Nevertheless, at the moment, as much as the beavers hated the Pig Farm, Foxwood and Pinchfield were far more dangerous foes. Like Foxwood and Pinchfield, the Pig Farm bombed the beaver dams. But unlike Foxwood and Pinchfield, the Pig Farm did not engage in hunting or trapping. More specifically, the Pig Farm did not engage in the horrific but highly profitable fur trade. Diso favored the assumption that this was merely an oversight of the pigs. Yet, Diso could not deny the undeniable—the Pig Farm had not been responsible for the continuing and senseless brutality. The Pig Farm was a newish regime, while, for as long as anyone could remember, Foxwood and Pinchfield had been relentless in their policy of stripping the Woodlands of every conceivable resource. A policy that was so far reaching as to peel the pelt from an animal's back. Just the previous season, nine beavers had been lost—to that vile, devilish pastime of transforming animals beautiful, brilliant, and loving, into coats.

Based upon this, through secret dispatches conveyed by Moses the raven, a tenuous alliance had been formed with the Pig Farm—an alliance that, however fragile, had lasted several seasons. Because of the swine's long-standing struggle against their neighbors (though the beavers saw hardly any difference between pork farmers and farmer pork), as well as their new association with a brilliant goat named Thomas, the Pig Farm had engineered revolutionary military technology.

Namely, they had devised a method to disable traps—spring-traps and others—by the use of kerosene bombs. Animal Farm had dispatched to the Woodlands special advisors, who would educate and advise the Woodlands animals on the mastery of this lifesaving technology. In exchange for this expertise, the beavers had conducted a covert war against Foxwood and Pinchfield. Instructed by the goats in tactical operations, the beavers learned not only the art of destroying the farmers' traps, but also the art of chewing holes in roofs, grain sheds, and chicken coops—and the art of mixing onion seed in the grass seed—and a dozen, dozen other such arts, which the beavers were all too happy to have their Woodlands adherents carry out.

IV

FILMONT ARRIVED HELPLESS. He was mostly Labrador, and part golden—all retriever. And having none of that fierceness that the shepherds of Animal Farm had, he had been beaten nearly to death by the farmer Frederick. The guard dogs had found him at the perimeter, bleeding from the mouth, and though they were initially shamed that any dog could be so passive, they could not but eventually be charmed by the shaggy tramp. He said he had never bitten anyone and he never would—he had never even been in a dogfight. And he would not even resist Frederick the farmer. He had just lain there under the man's swinging boot.

Filmont had been conveyed to the big barn on a scrapped door hitched to a steer. As most of the animals were then returning for the evening, Filmont had died before all of them—his body gone limp as his sandy-colored fur.

The last words that passed through his muzzle were words of love for his collie, Sandra-Marjorie, who was expecting a litter of puppies—his puppies.

Sandra-Marjorie was Mr. Pilkington's collie—Mr. Pilkington of Foxwood. And for this reason had Filmont been beaten by his own owner, Mr. Frederick, who, besides having a fondness for beating animals, was none too pleased to be informed by Mr. Pilkington that he would soon be receiving a litter of puppies—as his was the mongrel that fathered the mess. Frederick and Pilkington had always hated each other, and this romance of their dogs had exacerbated the situation. Nobody wanted a damn golden Labrador collie.

"Send a message to my Sandra-Marjorie," said Filmont, "that I will be waiting for her on the moon."

The scene was of such sentiment that many of the animals began to weep. For those unfamiliar with the lunar allusion, Norma the cat provided the salient belief of dog culture.

"Dogs think that when they die they go to the moon. That's why they always howl at the moon," she quietly explained.

Filmont exhaled his last, and the barn was penetrated by melancholy—that despair of life faced by death.

But then, Thomas the goat arrived.

"Clear the way! Clear the way!" cried Snowball—and the animals staggered aside to let the goat pass. There were puzzled snorts, clacks, and bleats as Thomas banged on the chest of the Labrador—and blew into his bleeding mouth. And then, suddenly, amid shocked whispers and cries, blood sputtered from Filmont's maw—and the dog heaved, and breathed again.

"Convey this dog to my laboratory!"

Months before, at the command of Thomas the goat, the old harness room had been transformed into a laboratory, where Thomas performed miracles of modern science. And it was here that Thomas performed his greatest miracle to date. One of the rats saw him do it, and reported back to the other animals in the middle of the night.

Thomas and Snowball had donned white uniforms and masks, whereupon, with the shiningest knife the rat had ever seen, Thomas the goat had cut open the dog's belly—

"Inside the dog, there were these different colored blobs, and one of them was bleeding. Thomas took some needle and thread and stitched it up, so it stopped bleeding," recalled the amazed rat—

"And then he stitched the dog closed. And, I think, the dog's still alive. And he's gonna stay alive."

And as it turned out, Filmont did survive.

His wound bandaged, the Labrador was given his own stall—where over the next weeks, he was visited by many of the animals, with whom he shared long conversations. Throughout his ordeal, his earnestness, his gentleness, endeared him to the farm animals.

Under the Pinchfield despot, Mr. Frederick, Filmont's life had been one hardship after another—and when he spoke of Animal Farm, of how the animals had taken control of their own lives, of the wonder represented by the voting process, of the miracle of education, and of how an animal could rise up, as had Napoleon, as had Snowball . . . well, he shared a dewy eye with many a creature. With no more than his own optimism, Filmont could renew a sense of Animal Farm greatness in beasts more accustomed to exhaustion. So encouraging, so without pretension (Yes, most animals were equalish!), Filmont could restore dignity to a rat who had not felt pride in his work since the day he switched from river to sewer, for the better hours. Here, in Filmont, was an animal who represented, merely by his arrival, what a glowing beacon Animal Farm was to the village. And here, in Filmont, was an animal that allowed all the farm animals, for at least a moment, to put aside their resentments of the newcomers who were digging under the fences to join the farm, and experience in their coming a reawakening of that initial freedom.

The animals had taken over the farm!

Ah yes, what glory! What limitless possibility!

Meanwhile, the re-education classes proceeded as scheduled—everyone was humanized. "Four legs good, two legs better," a few of the sheep remembered from somewhere. The geese were excused from the fields to work on providing the farm animals with clothing. Reams of cloth were delivered, and the geese took to their seamstress labors fairly capably. By the end of the summer, each male animal had one pair of short pants, one pair of long pants, one long-sleeved shirt, one short-sleeved shirt, and one headcloth—while each female had one short dress, one long dress, one shawl, and two bonnets. After the sewing was completed, the geese took up the laundry —as well as the patching and repairing of any garments that needed attention.

It was generally agreed that, really, clothing wasn't so bad— once a critter got used to it. Hot, a little bit, itchy, a little bit— but the animals appreciated the bright colors, and were soon bartering feed and services for more stylish vestments. It was supposed one might express one's individuality through an innovative bandanna.

As for the walking, some animals were more successful than others. The birds already had the two-legged gait down pat— and about half the sheep picked it up in the first week. Benjamin the donkey had no trouble—and as much as he complained about a pain in his left hip, he waddled with the best of them. The three horses, none of whom could recite the alphabet any higher than the letter B, found the task utterly impossible. Norma the cat, in contrast, lent a feline grace to the undertaking. The cows, too, adopted the form of locomotion without undue difficulty—though they did seem to do a good deal of leaning. The dogs, who with equal ease attained the upright position, were nevertheless allowed to remain on all fours most of the time—as they put forth a forceful argument that the bipedal position left them vulnerable and slow.

Likewise, with the help of Thomas the goat, the plans for the windmills were rapidly becoming a reality. A team of goat engineers had been brought in to fashion tools for animal paws (as opposed to human hands) and with a foundation of poured cement and cement blocks, the construction commenced in November. Utilizing wood planks milled at the old Napoleon Mill, the structures grew rapidly. For those who had any impression of the past, and the awful setbacks experienced by the workers of Animal Farm in building the Napoleon Mill, it certainly seemed as if that better world had finally arrived. Even the pigs were seen to work, now and again, at some extremely conspicuous task—but a task all the same. Snowball himself was known to distribute water.

"Pullin' my own weight," he would say, which was a good thing, as since his arrival he had put on several pounds. (He, Thomas, and several sows and nanny goats had taken up residence in the carriage house—the conversion of which was the very exemplification of animal elegance.)

Taken as a whole, the erection of the Twin Mills was not so much backbreaking and interminable as easy and fast. To facilitate the progress, the farm youth, in an act of enormous swine munificence, had been sent away to be educated—so frankly, it being the cold season, there wasn't much to do but work on the mills. (Without a litter to curl up with, what other way was there to keep warm?) The pigs were pleased to report that the Animal Farm coffers were holding out—and that it had not been deemed necessary to take out a "bank loan," whatever that might be, to complete the work. When the time came, experts were hired—and many of the animals found the presence of human electricians, welders, and inspectors disquieting. And yet, Snowball had been right—the walking on two legs and the wearing of clothing tended to diminish emotionalism on the part of human and animal alike. Many of the pigs had been so acclimated to humans, over their years of dealings with them, that the farm animals had trouble discerning any real difference between man and pig. (It often boiled down to nose vs. snout, shoes vs. hooves.) And as the days wore on, it was generally accepted that the best way to deal with a human was to treat it like a pig. They too appreciated a little toadyism.

The sad part of the construction was the accidental deaths of two animals. In the pouring of the concrete, one of the lambs had been lost. (He had been inadvertently nudged into the cement pit by a crowd of other sheep who were overly keen on watching the cement-pour up close.) The second loss, while no more tragic, was perhaps more acutely felt by the animals on the farm. Norma the cat had been electrocuted when her tail brushed a live wire. In respect for her sacrifice, the feline was not sold to the glue factory. (The remains of the lamb were not recovered.) Each of the two fatalities was distinguished with the honor, Animal Hero, Second Class.

To honor all the animals that had, since the rebellion, fallen in the service of the farm, the old Napoleon Mill was renamed. Snowball, at the March rededication, spoke of Boxer, a horse whom all now remembered (though they did seem to have previously forgotten him temporarily) as a giant of an equine, both in stature and spirit, who had worked himself to death for his love of Animal Farm, and his dream of a windmill that might make a better world.

"Henceforth," said Snowball, "the Napoleon Mill will be called—Dreamer's Mill."

This expressed, Filmont the Labrador became so excited that he started to chase his own tail—he just couldn't help it. And Snowball, with a benevolent gruntle, not only forgave the spectacle, but encouraged all the animals on the farm to follow the lead of Filmont, Boxer, and even Napoleon—

"Dream the impossible dream."

Concerning the completion of the Twin Mills, the only tinge of bitterness was that, following the inauguration, another Swiss goat had been brought in to initiate and oversee operations. (It would be nearly a year before any of that promised electricity and running water.) The outsider had been an associate of Thomas the goat—and as far as qualifications went, nobody could discern any, until the pigs printed a full-page biography, which differed pronouncedly from any rumored lack of qualifications. The position offered not only large rations and a room in the farmhouse (one needed to be well-fed and well-rested for brain work) but the respect afforded such an animalage.

It was soon decided, however, that the management of both mills was much too much for any one animal to accomplish— and when it was announced that a second animal would be chosen from among the farm animals to fill the position, the grumbling about the appointment of the Swiss goat (who was very qualified) largely subsided. The following Sunday Meeting, a competition was held between all who wished to fill the newly mandated managerial post. Presentations were mounted, and when the pigs and goats retired to confer upon the merits of the candidates, it was unanimously agreed among the farm animals that a bull by the name of Hobart had carried the day.

From the perspective of your average animal-in-the-barn, the contestants had been wildly varying in organization and intelligence—the low point, it was thought, being the nonsensical diagram scratched in the dirt by a chicken who, since the day she'd forgotten her own name, had been known around the farm as Temescula. "Temescula," she had decided, was a name so exotic she would never forget it. (This had turned out to be untrue, as Temescula regularly forgot she called herself

Temescula. "What's my name?" was her customary greeting.)
Nobody liked to hear bigoted talk, but Temescula was what
some animals would call a "chicken-head."

With the decision of the pigs and goats that Temescula had
been granted the post, there was an immediate reaction of
confusion and even anger. But when Pinkeye explained that
Temescula's diagram had been utterly brilliant, the animals
accepted the finding, as most of them were bright enough to
know they weren't bright enough to recognize brilliance.
(Besides that, Pinkeye's manner had been so honeyed and
earnest that no animal dared doubt him, lest they themselves
be considered devious.) Even Hobart merely shrugged, and
congratulated Temescula on her presentation.

The next day, the premiere issue of the Animal Farm weekly
newspaper, the *Daily Trotter*, was distributed.

"Local Fowl Makes Good!" declared the headline.

Those animals who could read (and the pigs so wanted
everyone to be able to read that enrollment in the literacy seminar was pushed up—fifty animals packed the classroom) were
treated to a marvelously moving biography of the chicken who
had, stubbornly, tirelessly, pursued several higher educational
degrees through a prestigious mail-order university.

"She always says yes," one of the pigs was quoted as saying—
"She's a can-do bird!"

Temescula, via a spokesrabbit, requested ten hours a week
of volunteer labor from each of the animals. Initially, added to
the extensive responsibilities of spring and summer, this was
toilsome indeed. But by September, after all the crops had
been harvested and brought to market, the hours seemed more
of a relief than a toil—as, aside from lending a paw to the
implementation of the electricity generated by the new windmills, there was little diversion to be had. The work would be

completed in January, it was hoped, and the heated stalls would go a good way to making the long winter short.

It was at the third meeting in October that Snowball put forth a plan to undertake, in the cool-weather lull, a possible annexation of the neighboring farms, Foxwood and Pinchfield, through something called a "lawsuit." When it was clarified that this was not another uncomfortable article of clothing, most of the animals seemed to think it was a good idea—as it required nothing of them.

But Minimus, who liked things the way they were, was not in agreement, and a debate ensued. Soon, said Minimus, they'd all have running water and electricity. Why get involved in the mania of the village? And even if they were to eventually get involved in the mania of the village, why not wait? With the Twin Mills, Animal Farm's position would surely get stronger.

Snowball, in reply, portrayed the lawsuit as retribution for old wrongs done Animal Farm, by Foxwood and Pinchfield. Minimus, in turn, claimed that lawyers were nothing more than a huge expense, and that no good ever came of them. Furthermore, he argued that Foxwood and Pinchfield were in such disrepair, and their populations in such poor health and of such poor education, that any annexation of those farms could serve Animal Farm no advantage. The animals of Animal Farm, he said, would be better off improving their own circumstance.

Not to be silenced, Snowball asserted that Foxwood and Pinchfield had been severely weakened by the beaver attacks that had become regular occurrences at both farms, and that now was the time to advance, not retreat.

"The enemies of Animal Farm are defenseless!"

Snowball raised his hooves—

"We must overwhelm them with every available means!"

And it was with this argument, and the enthusiastic cacophony of the animals in the barn, and the short bursts of bleat-bleating and oink-oinking from the goats and the pigs, that a strange look crossed Minimus's face. It was as if, though, of course, he was Prize Pig, he realized he was Prize Pig no longer. And as would ever more become the case at Sunday Meeting, he grew silent and surly.

The debate was reported at length in the *Daily Trotter*, where Minimus, in his sudden November turn-around, proclaimed that the concessions Snowball had made to his various concerns were more than enough to allay any fears. His faith in Snowball was complete—and every animal on the farm should feel exactly the same way. "Forward Ho!" proclaimed the *Daily Trotter*. In a letter-to-the-editor (penned by an excitable field mouse), it was suggested that the name Snowball was not forceful enough to capture the character of the visionary, and that perhaps "Snowstorm" would be more appropriate. The next week, Minimus showed up at the Sunday meeting looking like he had sat on a fretful porcupine. The *Trotter* reported that he was suffering a case of constipation. . . .

And when the hot water and showers and bathtubs and lights and electric heaters and air-conditioners were turned on—on January 14th—what a glorious day it was! What a glorious winter it was! And what a glorious spring it was! And what a hero Snowball was!

V

"TWO HUNDRED fresh pizza boxes!" exclaimed one of the rats.

And sure as slop, this was a time of plenty!

The castoff of the pigs' take-out food now littered every inch of the farm. It was almost impossible to look anywhere without seeing an empty bag of chips or a cookie box pushed into the ground. Also, as a residue of the human "experts" (plumbers and whatnot), there were beer cans and cigarettes everywhere. Additionally, due to the lack of suitable human potties (nobody wanted a human using their potty!), there were muddy mounds and yellow puddles wherever one stepped. The construction, too, had made its contribution—a lime pit, a scrap-heap mountain of rubber and plastic do-dads and broken bits, and, in the quarry, a pool of oil.

It was progress everywhere! said the pigs, to the cheers of the rats. It was civilization! And even a sheep was known to tip a beer bottle on end to drain those last delicious drops!

And all this, as the goats scientifically charted in the *Daily Trotter*—all this stinking blackness would enrich the soil, and make Animal Farm the most fertile farm in the land!

But really, there was no reason for that (enrichment, fertility) as there would be no crop come summer. It was not exactly that the animals were feeling lazy, or even sick—they were just feeling different. Maybe it was that now, in these good days, for the first time that any of them could remember, they were just enjoying the spring. Not even the pig overseers had ever before lain in the grass on a May afternoon, just to watch a beetle push a dung ball. So, simply stated, there was no farming, because there was no planting. Nobody seemed to want to plant, anymore.

Fortunately, Snowball and Thomas had introduced the pigs to the "sniff-test" for real money. And now confident in transactions of paper denominations, the pigs were enabled to hire out the Dreamer's Mill. In this, the animals managed to do their part, as limited as it was. Grind some grain. Cut some logs. Much better than pulling ploughs, all granted. Besides, there were far too many animals to work the mill everyday— so the activities were more distracting than obligatory.

Work when you want to. . . .

Filmont the Labrador loved these slow, warm days. Having long since recovered from his injuries, Filmont had established himself as not only an adept student of the humanization classes (he walked and wore clothing quite smartly) but as an able worker, when there was work to be done. With his ever-willingness to lend a paw, and his boundless generosity, he had become, perhaps, the most popular animal on the farm. (Except for Snowball—oh, and Minimus, by all means, not to forget Minimus.) And in those languorous days of spring and summer, Filmont wandered from stall to stall—and shared, with one animal and the next, long draughts from buckets of water, which he frequently flavored with a few drops of whiskey. And he and his hosts would talk of their loves and pains—and then, in graceful transition, the animals would sit back, and listen to Filmont as he dreamily reminisced of the places he had been when he was a pup.

Filmont had once been loved by a girl named Madeline Frederick (whom he had not seen in so long that he assumed she was dead) and she had brought him absolutely everywhere. He spoke of carnivals and fairgrounds. And even a circus that he had watched while sitting on the young lady's lap—he'd been rolled up in her sweater. Bless her soul, he would sigh, those were the days—cotton candy and smoked sausage and turkeys roasted on skewers. "Oh, excuse me," he'd apologize to any pig that might be in hearing distance, or bird who might take offense. But even so—entirely disregarding the meat—he described a place of leisurely distraction that eclipsed all of life's miseries. And the animals, without so much as setting a hoof in such a paradise, did indeed experience a forgetting—a blissful release from their every woe.

Yes, there could be a light-hearted laugh! Yes, there could be a light-hearted land!

And when Filmont remembered the song that his Madeline had sung to him as she cradled him in her arms, well, it didn't take long before he had howled himself hoarse and, in his stead, the other animals were taking up the old folk melody— some called it a spiritual—to harmonize as they sat around the campfire, roasting earthworms.

I went to the Animal Fair. The birds and the beasts were there,
The big raccoon, by the light of the moon, was combing his
*   auburn hair.*
The monkey he got drunk, and fell on the elephant's trunk,
The elephant sneezed, and fell on his knees,
And that was the end of the monk! The monk! The monk!
*   The monk!*

And as it turned out, Snowball too was listening—to Filmont and the animals. And Snowball too was learning— from Filmont and the animals. And it was in mid-June, the first item on the agenda of a Sunday Meeting, that Snowball proposed his own carnival, which, to the oohs and ahhs of half a dozen campfire regulars, he called, "Animal Fair." (Several of the sheep, who immediately started out, "*We went to the Animal Fair . . .*" were quieted with a few sharp nips by a pair of shepherds who, perhaps, had been appointed for this very contingency.)

Snowball's proposition was to open the farm—

"Open the farm to the village, as, when we erected our windmills, we opened the farm to the wind."

"Our lives," said Snowball, "will be easy. Our profits large —our expenses low. Where now there are trees—tomorrow, lights. Glowing electric lights like ten million fireflies. Animal Farm will become Animal Fair—a land where dreams come true. Hot baths, air-conditioning—have we not made our own dreams come true? We have! So now, let us help to make everyone else's dream come true. It will be, not just an amusement park, but a wondrous demonstration of the pure spirit of the animal! We will share with all the village—our own magic! And from it, we will feed not only our renown, but our stomachs, and the stomachs of our young—as our vision rewards us with every conceivable animal comfort!"

To this, there were honks, snorts, and grunts all around, and the sheep burst out, "Animal comfort! Animal comfort!"

Over the clamor and natter, Minimus asserted his disagreement. But his arguments seemed so feeble (as he seemed so feeble—that old fat pig) so as to be almost nonexistent. He called the carnival a zoo. Snowball's retort that Animal Fair would not be a zoo, that it would not be a zoo at all, was gratefully received by the animals. They understood the theme park as Snowball saw it—an educational resort that would spread the word, and teach the village, about the victories of Animal Farm, and the lives of animals free!

Minimus, glowering through his jowls, was not convinced—though the resistance he offered was marginal. Truth
be told, Minimus was increasingly marginalized himself.
Snowball, with his educated goats and the support of the next
generation of pigs, was firmly placed at the nexus of decision-
making. Minimus, meanwhile, had moldered, gone mushy—
not only in the flesh, but in the brain. Though it was seldom
discussed, Minimus was often noticed, during Sunday
Meeting, dozing off at the most crucial moments.

So, Snowball had wrested power from Minimus. So,
Minimus had become Snowball's rival. All that was clear but
. . . So what? Minimus was no more than a specter—a shadowy
figure at the rear of the barn. And yet, there remained some
undercurrent of nervousness, as surely one could not ignore
Minimus entirely. Though zizzing pacifically at his place
along the back wall, Minimus was still flanked by the power-
hungry Pinkeye, and the I'll-eat-anyone-if-you-give-me-the-
order Brutus. . . .

At the first Sunday Meeting of December, it was resolved
that the farm should undertake the ambitious project of the
fair—and Snowball (his approval ratings at an all-time high)
told the animals what he would need.

He would need all the eggs laid by the chickens—and he
would need them for some time to come.

To every species but the chickens, the justification that the
farm had exhausted its resources on the Twin Mills seemed a
reasonable one. Though profitable, the Mills had not yet paid
off the "bank loan" that had, in the end, been taken out to fund
the construction. As Snowball explained it, a "bank loan" was
like borrowing something from a friend, but the something
was money, and the friend was the bank. Currently, the mon-
eys generated by the mills were only enough to repay that

friend. The chicken eggs would be used to finance a new loan, which in turn would be used to finance Henron, a collectively owned pig and hen corporation (the pigs would take on the onerous task of administration), which in turn would be used to finance the amusement park. He was sorry, Snowball told the chickens, but milling grain and lumber just wouldn't pay the bills.

It was in silence that the black Minorca hens toddled from the Sunday Meeting. And it was in silence, without a peep of justification, that they rebelled—as they had in Napoleon's time. The eggs already in their nests—they pushed out. They would have considered it barbaric to sell them for food, as close to hatching as those eggs had been. Their new eggs— they laid on the slanted roof of their coop. The eggs would roll down the shingles and smash on the packed ground—financing nothing, and hatching for no blushing Minorca mother.

Snowball did not apply force to the chickens, as had Napoleon years before. Minimus, harkening to Napoleon, and briefly backed by popular opinion (the animals wanted that park!), argued for starving them out. But where Napoleon had ceased their rations, Snowball increased them, and congratulated the chickens on their independence—whereupon, with the encouragement of one chicken in particular (who was suddenly wearing an exquisitely tailored red-knit afternoon suit) the birds began to lose their resolve. Upon return to her nesting box, each chicken, courtesy of Henron, found a shortbread cookie.

The next matter was that of filling the high-level managerial positions necessary to an amusement park. As always, in the presentations, Hobart the bull was spectacular. So forthright, so knowledgeable—it was always said of the popular bull, "surely Hobart has won this time!"

But it was never Hobart.

The first winner, who had gained the position of Master Mason, was a chicken who had not managed to lift her brick. It was iterated in the *Trotter* that, as an overseer, she would not be required to lift bricks, and that her theoretical knowledge of the subject was, in toto, detailed and extensive. Yet, excepting the pigs and goats, her statement that bricks were "hard red blocks" left few impressed. It immediately went about the farm that there was a predisposition to chickens—indeed, that Temescula herself had been chosen because the pigs and goats knew they would soon require the henhouse eggs, and that this Mason bird had been assigned because the pigs and goats still needed them.

Always alert to farm gossip, the pigs and goats emphatically denied the slanderous slur. An editorial in the *Trotter* asked if it had not once been whispered that the goats had given out positions based upon nepotism—and, further queried the essay, had that assertion not been proven false? And yes, agreed those animals who could read (and moreover, knew what "nepotism" meant) yes, it was true that it had not only been goats who were appointed, as the last two managerial appointees had been, undeniably, chickens. And, asked a follow-up op-ed several weeks later, had not the Twin Mills been functioning at levels of peak efficiency under the two managers that had been chosen? Well yes, agreed the animals (who had wearied of having their own opinions, as having one's own opinion seemed to mean dedicating every respite to the endlessly grueling endeavor of making sense of the *Daily Trotter*) yes, they supposed that was also so. . . .

Temescula knew for a fact it was so. In response to questions about her work schedule, the hen was quoted in the *Trotter* as saying that she was so efficient she didn't need to go to work to do her job. (Since her posting, she'd become what some of the geese called "arrogant.") It was commonly disbelieved by the animals on the farm that Temescula, as she claimed, invented water. Neither the pigs nor the goats had any comment.

In the following weeks, to further disprove any allegation of malfeasance in the managerial selection process, the animals posted were of every variety. A sheep was given the "Innovative Design" position. A bat and a mole, jointly, were appointed to the "Scenic Vistas" position. And, rather startlingly, a woodpecker was appointed to the "Structural Engineering" position.

Always, it must be said, Hobart presented superbly—although, sadly, as the pigs were all so fond of Hobart, he just never seemed to "cut the mustard."

Still, for the "Rousing the Village" position, it seemed that Hobart had again carried the day. Filmont the Labrador, competing for the first time, also made an excellent presentation, and as Filmont had such a charming manner and excellent way of relating to animals and people alike, and what's more, such an intense love and loyalty for the farm, some held that he would attain the post. His demeanor over the weeks previous to the posting presentations had been so very upbeat and generally genial that he had earned the designation, "Filmont the if-you-just-have-a-positive-attitude Labrador." But, as always, a surprise was in store for the speculators, as the public-relations title was pawed off to a sheep named Elsworth, who had never had much to say (not even in his presentation), but an oh-so enthusiastic and friendly—

"What ho?"

Some discussion immediately followed as to whether the bestest animal had been chosen. Thomas the goat reminded the animals that public relations was not about being the bestest, but instead, the chipperestest, which this sheep, Elsworth, was. And Snowball remarked how excellent the sheep were, as evidenced during the construction of the Twin Mills, at crowd control. Everybody tried to remember that—but couldn't. Though Benjamin surely remembered, as usual, he had nothing to say, so the animals, hearing from Snowball that this was the case, quite naturally assumed that it was true. True as cool rain on a hot day.

But that night, that very Sunday of his appointment, Elsworth was bitten on the neck, bled to death from his jugular vein, and partially devoured by an unknown culprit. The body was found at dawn. The murder—the first like it that anyone remembered—would never be solved. "(What Ho?" read the headline of the *Trotter*.) It was hypothesized that the culprit was some lone wolf, who had committed the senseless act of violence for no reason better than that he was passing through. A cow named Bell, who had, fittingly enough, dedicated her life to the study of all the different bells that a cow might wear (brass, iron, or steel), replaced the fallen sheep in the coveted position. Bell was given a cowbell of solid silver. And that, said the pigs, was publicity! The sheep was made Animal Hero, Seventh Class, and the remainder of his corpse was sent to the butcher. He would, as the pigs put it, have wanted it that way.

The next position filled was that of "Scout," and the appointing of this post was perhaps the first that any of the animals could fathom. The assignment was given to a pigeon who scoured the countryside for the future animal attractions of the park. As was typical of his species, the bird was quite outgoing—conducting interviews at every crossroads, he easily covered eight circular miles a day. Thus, it was straightway that discoveries were made, freedoms were bought, and performers were en route to their new home—Animal Farm, soon to be Animal Fair!

Among the newcomers, was a pleasing and attractive donkey by the name of Emerald. She was not a young animal, but not old either—and had a mother's air of kindness and wisdom. Her young son, Kip, was a somewhat unsteady youth—as he had never known his father. Benjamin, normally touched by nothing, showed a generosity to the pair that would have been thought previously impossible. He was so solicitous of the mother and son that some of the more sentimental geese openly wept for his kindness shown the lone mother and her fatherless child.

And it was not just the geese—Emerald too was moved by old Benjamin's gentleness. It had been several years since, besides her son, she had even seen another donkey.

Emerald, a mathematical genius, could solve any mathematical question a human could pose. And the animals looked forward to the day she would perform—that would show those humans that an animal was just as good as they were! Though not what the *Trotter* referred to as a "headliner," Emerald would be one of the many entertainers in the "tradeshow," which would make up the majority of the fair's attractions—the performers fulfilling roles ranging from solving mathematical theorems, such as the case of Emerald, to removing mislocated bubble gum from hair or fur, such as the case of a one-winged duck who went by the name Worm.

Everyone could be a part of the triumph!

And, as everybody anticipated everybody's triumph, solidarity on the farm rose to an all-time high. Animal Fair was sung with unsurpassed vigor . . . that is, until a shocking discovery was made by one of the rats. The blueprints for the Twin Mills had been sold to Mr. Frederick of the Pinchfield

Farm. And probably, the blueprints had been sold by an animal! Despite an extensive investigation, the identity of this betrayer-of-all-animals was not determined. Yet, apparent as it may have seemed that the security of the Twin Mills had been compromised, the pigs argued persuasively that Mr. Frederick was already under court order not to set foot on Animal Farm—and that the legal (hence financial) repercussions of either him or Pilkington sallying forth a single toe onto the grounds would be so severe as to thwart even the most stalwart enemy. (And it would certainly be enough to thwart either one of those poorhouse jellyfish!)

Minimus, however, who felt he'd put up with far too much already, had reached his breaking point. He was inconvincible—unmovable. And, over this issue of the traitor, his clash with Snowball was felt more profoundly than on any previous occasion. Snowball, who advocated further investigation by the dogs, saw no immediate danger to Animal Farm—and, thusly, no reason to stir up unneeded anxiety. (Who needed unneeded anxiety?) Minimus, conversely, who could feel nothing but the hot breath of a traitor in his midst, wanted to submit every last farm animal to interrogation—until the conspirator had been exposed and brought to justice. Justice being the jagged fangs of the shepherds. In short, Minimus wanted the traitor torn to pieces, and promptly—while Snowball was more concerned with other projects.

"Animal Fair must go on," Snowball said—

"Don't stop working, and don't worry. We'll take care of it."

And that's exactly what happened—the animals didn't stop working, they didn't worry, and whatever the outcome might be (surely a good one), they entrusted the matter of their personal safety to the canines and swine.

Minimus, who was unable to go forward with such mightiness as he so desperately desired, was nevertheless put in charge of the ongoing operation—investigative and defensive. The Prize Pig took to wearing a military-style helmet—and dubbed himself the Universal Protector.

VI

KEROSENE TECHNOLOGY had been a colossal boon for the beavers—their science was thriving, and the loss of life from the spring-traps had been substantially diminished. Furthermore, it was felt that the kerosene anti-traps were doing their part, however limited, to undo the enemy—the human farms of Pinchfield and Foxwood. The Pig Farm had been making inroads with its lawsuits, as well, and it was not inconceivable that the evil regimes might someday topple.

On the other paw, the continuing problem of who controlled the stream had placed a stranglehold (a leash!) on Woodlands economy and culture. Rather than destroy a new dam, the Pig Farm had tendered a substantial sum to the beavers to allow the free flow of water. The acceptance of this remuneration, clearly, had been a compromise of the Ancient Beaver Code, and gravely injurious to the identity of the beavers—yet the income was indispensable to the beavers if they wished to achieve their long-term goal. The return to the Ancient Beaver Code.

To this end, prairie dog and meerkat advisors were brought in to oversee the enlargement of the bunkers, and the active components of the kerosene bombs (kerosene and gunpowder) were stockpiled. The beavers, whose extensive families attended to the dealings of these materials, did not benefit from the trade. This was made abundantly clear on the

Woodlands, megaphone-format news broadcast, Beaveada—
"Beavers do not benefit from the kerosene trade." The
beavers simply lived in better conditions than the other
Woodlands animals, and ate better food, and had resources to
throw around. This, fortunately, as it was always a comfort to
think that if one found oneself starving to death, there was at
least a chance that some plump shining beaver, rigorous in
the support of Woodlands followers of the Ancient Beaver
way, might come along and drop a sack of meal somewhere
nearby, into which, there was also the possibility, one might
burrow one's snout, if one was quick, before such sack was
entirely emptied . . .

For, by and large, assets being so limited, the average
Woodlands animals didn't have much to show for the Pig
Farm disbursements. In truth, being the ones who had to
actually implement the kerosene anti-trap units, the
Woodlands animals were working longer hours than ever.
And those anti-trap units were a dangerous business, besides.
Sometimes, following a faulty or unexpected kerosene detona-
tion, an animal entirely disappeared, leaving no more, for
example, than an aroma of weasel. Diso, on Beaveada, praised
the soldiers their heroics.

Still, it was only natural that questions arose, albeit in
hushed undertones, as to whether this kerosene technology
wasn't actually some breach of the hallowed Beaver Code.
Diso, firm on this point, issued assurances that any defensive
act (namely, springing a potentially murderous spring-trap)
was in no way at odds with the code. And to assuage not only
the theological fears of the doubters (or "ye of no faith"), but
also the more definite fears of those who risked self-annihila-
tion, incineration, laceration, indentation, or the more general
truncation, which might, or might not, be facilitated by

amputation, Diso alluded to the 1600 virgin saplings which awaited believers—especially those who died for the right reasons, such as setting off spring-traps. (Those uninspired by talk of a Lodestar undulating with virgin birch saplings were assured of 1600 fresh caterpillars, or 1600 blackberry bushes, or 1600 fly maggots or earwig eggs—according to one's palate.)

So, some believed, some believed fervently, some didn't believe, and some didn't believe fervently, but for the most part, the Woodlands animals couldn't be bothered with belief—instead, they just did what they were told. Diso and his officers were not too tolerant of anything else. Hesitation. Dissent. When, trodding along the happy trail, one encountered some disemboweled water vole trailing ten feet of intestines from an eight-foot tree—well, there was someone who bothered to believe.

And so, as for the ongoing war against Foxwood and Pinchfield, while the beavers felt better spiritually and intellectually equipped for victory, the Woodlands animals felt better motivated for it. To the Woodlands animals, victory meant conclusion—and, unlike defeat, a conclusion that put an end to the dreaded fur traps, and all the horrors those traps engendered. Lest anyone forget who was to blame for the woes of the Woodlands animals, Beaveada was continually publicizing reports of mothers, fathers, sons, and daughters, who had twisted off their own limbs to escape the steel jaws of doom. Equally tragic, if not more so, were the tales of the other pitiable unfortunates, who, preferring to end their agony, made no attempt at escape—and rather, in excruciating pain, just waited for their human executioners to arrive. Sometimes, they waited a week.

As inflamed as the beavers were already, it was with his typical inflammatory rhetoric that Moses enlightened the beavers on how well the animals on the Pig Farm were living—without a single one of them even believing in the Sugarcandy Lodestar! Though perhaps luxurious to the other Woodlands animals, the lifestyle of the beavers, in comparison to the pigs, was one of bare subsistence. Despite the garden salads, roasted nuts, and freshly pressed beet-juice, the beavers believed that life was essentially hard—and only to be relieved, upon death, by an ascent to that sweet Lodestar in the sky.

But while the beavers were in the woods abstaining (no pie) so that they might in the afterlife attain glory, the farm animals were enjoying hot baths and electric heaters—without adhering to any code at all. The farm animals were hedonists who sat around passing gas. (Actually, the beavers were quite right, as any reckless dispersal, including one of methane, was a sure quantification of success to a pig.)

On the horizon, the beavers could see the Twin Mills, towering above all the surrounding area. There they were—the Twin Mills, in ceaseless relief, in ceaseless reminder. The beavers could not look away. The Twin Mills—the object not only of their own wealth, but of their own oppression. They stared—envious and self-righteous, enraged and determined.

Over the next few months, many of the moles, mice, squirrels, rabbits, frogs, and other Woodlands animals (who weren't nearly so unwavering or resentful) abandoned the Woodlands in favor of emigrating—to join the farm. The Pig Farm. It seemed that the notion of starting anew, in a heated stall, could be overwhelming. It was common knowledge that the Pig Farm animals were fat, lazy, and spoiled—and to compound this with the idea that, on the Pig Farm, one could succeed by hard work . . . it was just too much for the common mole to resist. (I *already work hard*, such a mole would think, *and I can certainly work harder than an animal who's fat, lazy, and spoiled*.) In the Woodlands, it was often said of the Pig Farm animals that they were so brainless and inept that they could chew off three legs—and still be caught in the trap. And thus, families were gathered up, cheeks were packed with seeds and acorns, and muffled oaths of "no more digging" were made.

And the Woodlands animals who remained behind would just squat on the big rock and stare at the Twin Mills—towering over the village. And, so squatting, so staring, the Woodlands creatures would either grow more resentful, and ardent about the beaver's way, or more committed to migrating to that better land.

The beavers, too, squatted and watched. Often, up on the big rock, they were joined by Moses, who expounded passionately on the subject of the Epoch of the Beaver, and recalled to the beavers their sacred ways. To die for the cause of the Ancient Beaver Code, said Moses with a tremulous caw, would send an animal straight to the Sugarcandy Lodestar—that oasis of light in the night sky, where days were as carefree as the days of pups, and fruit was always in season, and honeybees had no stingers.

Under the guidance of Moses, the beavers were becoming more devout—their beaver pride balanced only by their anger. The animals on the Pig Farm were now walking on two legs. The beavers, so staunch in their beaver ways, were incensed. Two legs bad, four legs good, Moses had told them—and everyone knew besides, that this was an ancient truth of all animals.

Soon after, the birds of the Woodlands, so as to be walking on all fours, were forced to volunteer to drag their wingtips when they walked.

VII

ANIMAL FARM was building a carnival—a showcase of electric lights, edifying spectacles, and delights to the senses. As effortlessly as the locality had watched the Twin Mills erected, the theme park was going up even easier—even faster. There was no denying it now—Animal Farm was a runaway success. Not only did it have one of the highest standards of living for any farm, it was a farm that promised freedom—and, moreover, with the carnival under way, a thousand opportunities. Clear-cutting the Woodlands for lumber and land—pumping black smoke into the air from the electrical plant that was motored by the Twin Mills—there was industry in the air!

And it was attracting new animals like bees to honey!

There were moles, voles, hedgehog, shrews, mice, rats, squirrels, weasels, rabbits, porcupines, foxes, toads, frogs, lizards, snakes, pigeons, ducks, geese, and the badgers, who, an extremely boisterous lot, were liked by all, except the voles, whose introverted personalities left them at odds with the grub-eating extroverts, whom they considered brusque, loud, and foolish. Of course, there were many other types of animals, and there were many other types of feuds and rivalries—some rooted in past grievances, some utterly new. And just as there were animals that were popular, the gregarious badgers, for example, there were animals that were unpopular, such as the rats. No matter how often the *Trotter* described the farm's vermin residents as upfront, thorough, and absolutely indispensable to the general clean-up and presentability of the park, the *Rattus rattus* community could not shake a reputation for being dirty and shiftless.

As for specific animosities, the cows and horses had it in for the snakes. (After that trampling incident in the barn, which had, accidental as it was, nearly cost one innocent snake his life, the hard feelings directed at the snakes by the cows and horses turned mutual—and the snakes directed those feelings back.) The chickens could not forgive the foxes the offences of their fathers—much as the rabbits could not forgive the dogs the offences of theirs. For reasons all too obvious, nobody wanted to have much to do with the porcupines, who were likable enough creatures, if you got to know them, but still, not the kind of friend you wanted to cuddle up with. The bats, who worked the night shifts, weren't too well regarded either. The beavers, as well, raised a few ears, as private, even standoffish, as those long-toothed creatures were.

Some, as a rule, viewed the newcomers as a shady and angry lot—while others strongly disagreed. The pigs had little to contribute to this debate—they merely reiterated in their regular press releases that, as was continually evidenced by their appointments to official positions, they embraced animal diversity. Nevertheless, it did seem to be an accepted fact that there was a tendency for newcomers to be unfamiliar with the ways of the farm. Although this was only to be expected, many of the farm animals no longer remembered how difficult it had been for them, when they were learning how to walk and wear clothing. (Occasionally, one heard a meanspirited joke about the "dumbcomers," such as—*why don't dumbcomers take work-breaks that last longer than fifteen minutes? Because they don't want to get retrained*.)

But, regardless of obstacles, the newcomers did learn to walk and wear clothing—and after a time, they became as accustomed to it as anyone else. And whatever an animal said, it could not be denied that, for the most part, the newcomers consisted of hard workers. Indeed, most of them had come to work, specifically, at those jobs the original farm animals would no longer perform. Empty and sanitize the human bathrooms, clean the windows of the big barn. . . . It was difficult not to admire some of the newcomers, actually, for this work ethic, as many of them were far too educated to attend such tasks. What's more, to live in those makeshift shacks on the marshy side of the field . . .

Well . . . to live there, with no hot water or electricity, that was a determined lot.

Well . . . mostly.

There were the ostriches—the six eggs having been purchased from a local farmer who claimed that ostriches were too ornery to breed. It had been thought that such exotic animals would surely make an excellent exhibit for the carnival. But the ostriches, too dumb to understand they were free, were always trying to escape. A dog pack was assigned as an escort—not only to protect the farm's investment, but to protect the ostriches from themselves (an ostrich on its own would be totally unable to attend such basic needs as health and shelter). On the open field, however, the ostriches regularly broke away from their protectors—and easily outpaced them. What they thought they would accomplish by this truancy was an obscure matter, as, invariably, the birds would just run into the electric fence, where they would fall, unconscious, into the fringe of ostrich down that ringed the farm.

The charred birds were an ongoing unpleasantness. *There goes another stupid ostrich. Is he gonna run? Looks like he fell face first onto a griddle*. A discussion ensued in the *Trotter* as to whether the ostriches really were trying to get somewhere/do something, or they just liked the electric fence. It was sometimes postulated that this continuing barbeque was, among the ostriches, a contest of strength. Who could smack the fence hardest? Who could endure the volts longest?

After all the pigs had done for them! Those dumb ostriches!

To spare everyone the spectacle, the ostriches were moved off to a housing area on the outskirts of the farm. And as that area was enclosed with its own electric fence, there was no more of the nasty business—aside from the periodic THWPT, and subsequent THUMP of some 345-pound bird. Over the top of the fence, there would be a plume of sparks and feathers.

Those less forbearing among the pigs had been especially infuriated by the needless, senseless disgrace. Outspoken among the irate—Minimus. And by way of the Prize Pig's wrath, which took the form of an editorial published in the *Trotter*, a resentment towards all new animals was promptly precipitated from the general population—as everybody already had his or her own hostilities toward the newcomers.

Some of the farm animals called for the expulsion, posthaste, of all newcomers. And yet, several of the newcomers were so loved that nobody, not even those who called for immediate action, could bear to see them go. How could anyone say good-bye to Emerald the counting donkey, or her son, Kip? Besides, many of the newcomers, like Emerald, had special abilities, while others were performing labors that nobody else would perform. In rebuttal, naysayers among the original animals argued that no job held by a newcomer couldn't be filled by one of their own, and that as for special abilities—those could be taught to the original animals who wanted to learn them.

It was perhaps Minimus who phrased it best, in his self-published pamphlet —

ANIMAL FARM FOR FARM ANIMALS

At the first Sunday Meeting that followed Minimus's distribution of his pamphlet, Pinkeye, fulfilling his duties as Next Prize Pig, called for a vote among farm animals (the original animals, that is, who were the only animals allowed to vote) on whether or not to keep the newcomers. It would be all or nothing — either force the newcomers to go, now, or let them stay, forever. Should the newcomers be permitted to remain, they would be entirely recognized as animals of the farm, and even be extended the right to vote on those issues that the animals typically voted on — such as whether or not to paint the barn doors red. (The farm animals, who had never before voted on an issue like immigration, were pleased to perceive themselves so much a part of the process.)

Before the ballots were cast on the fate of the newcomers, Minimus spoke of how many rats were among the assortment, and how the rats had historically been in league with the enemies of Animal Farm. And as the animals looked to the rats (the mice, too, for that matter) they could see that, indubitably, there was something disreputable about them. Making the case for the opposition, Snowball spoke of how all animals wanted a chance — and how he wanted to be a part, and he wanted Animal Farm to be a part, of giving them that chance.

A goat instructed the voters — "yes" for stay, "no"' for go.

"Yes for stay, no for go," repeated the sheep.

And then, in the usual manner, the goats made their way through the barn, and the animals turned in their ballots. The goats, carrying note pads, read off the votes as they counted them.

"Yes."

"No."

"Yes."

"No."

"No."

"Yes."

Dozens of baa-ing voices filled the barn. How the goats kept track of it all was beyond anyone—though in only a few minutes the votes were tallied.

"The numbers are in," said Snowball, who stood atop his soapbox as he read from a note pad—

"One hundred and eighty-three votes—yes. One hundred and eighty-three votes—no."

What did this mean? wondered the animals. And they whispered to each other—

"It's a tie. A tie!"

"Yes," Snowball raised his hooves in his characteristic gesture—

"It's a tie. But one animal hasn't yet voted."

The animals exhaled—

Who? Who hasn't voted? Who will cast the deciding ballot?

It was Filmont the Labrador who first apprehended the abstainer—

"Benjamin."

And all the animals, especially the geese, whispered to each other—

"Benjamin!"

"Benjamin!"

"Benjamin!"

And Snowball pointed his hoof—

Benjamin!

All looked to the donkey, who, standing in his stall, had lowered his head and closed his eyes.

Benjamin had always refused to do much of anything in connection with decision-making on the farm. He would just say that this was a hard life, and resume whatever he'd been doing. Certainly, he had always refused to vote. True, the issues before had been minor—such as where to plant the flowerbed, or how high the water fountain should spout water. (Come to think of it, nothing serious had ever been put to a vote. No, the animals shook their heads, that must be wrong. They just didn't remember.) But even so—even with a ballot so momentous as this, would Benjamin vote?

Would he cast the tie-breaking vote?

"Benjamin?" posed Snowball.

Benjamin stood beside his new friend (his new, close friend), Emerald the counting donkey, and her son, Kip, both of whom, along with the rats, squirrels, badgers, bats, and all the others newcomers, were dependent upon the outcome of this vote for their very futures.

Emerald and Kip looked to Benjamin with watery eyes— Benjamin looked to Emerald and Kip with watery eyes.

And then the old donkey raised his ears and his muzzle. And the whole barn inhaled, as if to wonder—

What—yes for stay, or no for go?

And, at long last, a stream of tears running off the end of his nose, Benjamin exercised his suffrage—

"Yes, they stay. They all stay."

Emerald nuzzled Benjamin affectionately. Kip nuzzled Emerald. And all the animals who wanted the newcomers to stay let out a cheer. And all the animals who wanted the new-comers to go let out a groan. And the newcomers—they let out a sigh. And then it was over. And after singing *Animal Fair*, which had now officially replaced *Beasts of Earth*, the Meeting was dismissed.

The next day, a number of the geese, who, coincidentally, made up the majority of Minimus's kitchen staff, proceeded from the Jones House to the barnhouse, where they mounted a cantankerous and clamorous protest. *Animal Farm for farm animals!* Patently opposed to opening the farm to the newcomers, they complained that they had been skipped over in the counting. Emerald (recently voted in with the other newcomers) was consulted, as it was known she could count anything without even trying, and she would undoubtedly know if the figures cited by the goats had been correct. But Emerald, in a sad way, answered that the scene had been just too overwhelming, and . . . she hadn't counted. She was sorry.

Minimus was not available for comment, reported the *Trotter*.

For the newly legitimized immigrants, a new classroom was built—and a new lesson was established. In this classroom, with this lesson, over the next seven weeks, these newcomers were initiated—told what Animalism was, and what the flag meant, et cetera.

"This flag represents our boundless faith in Animal Farm," repeated the new farm animals, holding their mitts to their pumping hearts and proudly droning the words they would drone for forty-nine consecutive days—

"The green represents the enormous bounty that the village offers—fields of clover for everyone! And the hoof, horn, and wing represent how we're all working together for a great future. It doesn't matter if we're purple, yellow, or orange, this village is our village!"

"Also," shrieked a rat who was a bit too eager at the swear-in, which was conducted at the historic site of the old tar wall, "the green represents money! Money, money, money!"

Inappropriate as this outburst was, it expressed the genuine emotions of many of the farm animals, and new farm animals —as, for some time, there had been rumors that every one of them (not just the goats and pigs) would soon have money at their pad-tips. That all animals pawdle money, it was reasonably assumed, was a prerequisite for opening an amusement park —so this rumor had been granted considerable credence. And while the rat said, "Money, money, money!" so too thought many of the animals, even if they weren't exactly sure what money consisted of, or what it would do for them.

To house the new animals, who had been camping in the weeds on the marshy side of the field, it was decided that a new barn should be built. The animals original to the farm would take up residence in these new barracks, as it would offer many amenities, while the new arrivals would occupy the old barnhouse, which, it was duly noted, was really not so bad—after all, not many of the émigrés had ever enjoyed such luxuries as hot and cold running water, bathtubs, windows, air-conditioning, heating, and electricity, even if the original farm animals had become curiously accustomed to that sort of thing.

The new stalls were erected as efficiently as anything else the farm had put up. And soon enough, Animal Farm had a new barnhouse (as well as a new lime pit, and a new pile of debris).

The cement stalls of the new barracks offered an opulence heretofore unimaginable. Although each stall was about half the size, in square feet, of a comparable stall in the old barn, these stalls were architecturally innovative—the floor plan consisted of an L-shaped design. Additionally, every stall was equipped with its own flush toilet! And not only that—each stall was furnished with a feather mattress, a looking glass, a horsehair sofa, and a lithograph of one's own choosing! Of course, it did take considerable resources, and another loan had to be taken out on the farm. Also, three ducks and a cow were killed during the construction (two accidents with the earthmover, and one with the crane). But to have these accouterments, in addition to the bathtubs and windows and stall-to-stall carpeting that they all took for granted . . . well that was a good enough reason to die, or take out a loan—as terrifying and mysterious as death or financing might be.

The new barracks was named the Thomas Tower (after Thomas the goat), and was launched into service with a smashed bottle of champagne, and a can of fruit cocktail for everyone.

And it was right at the peak of these goodest good times, that a new crisis shook Animal Farm. But this crisis, as full of intrigue as any of those that had come to Animal Farm since Snowball's arrival, was also full of peril, and violence. . . .

Fall had come, and as the usual Sunday Meeting gathered, the animals spoke of how beautiful it was to see the turning of the trees (of the few trees there were). Off in the distance, they could see the hills—leafy oceans of red, yellow, and green rolled in the wind. And just as the animals were settling into this bucolic mood, and stepping into the barn, they saw Minimus, who had not been seen for some time, flanked by a pack of snarling, salivating dogs.

Dogs, to be sure, were always snarling and salivating, but anyone could see how different this was. And as Snowball walked through the big doors into the barn, the animals could see the reason. And Snowball could see the reason.

"Dogs!" rumbled Minimus, his tone low and commanding— "Sic 'im!"

For a long time Animal Farm had been two things. The one way—and the other. Minimus and Snowball. But now, all the animals understood, be it verbally or instinctually, that this was the end of the long brotherly hatred—that the old war was over.

And with Minimus's order, there came sudden motion—
harried voices. And Brutus and his dogs were charging—and
the animals were scattering. Directions were chosen—every
which way—though nobody knew which was the way to safety, or if there was such a way. There was pushing. There was
shoving.

"Follow me!"

"No, follow me!"

"Get out of my way!"

"No, get out of mine!"

There was the drawing of lines in the sand—there was the
crossing of those lines. There was squawking, hissing, and
baring of teeth. There was backbiting, and kicking. There was,
all over, that kind of turmoil that can only come from not
knowing, not having even the dimmest of suspicions, as to
what the hour would bring.

One turtle, having finally surmounted the mêlée, was
pushing forth through the barn doors—perhaps hoping to
take shelter in the rock pile by the barn. And there, as she
passed through the gravel, she and a growing number of
farm animals saw that there—out there in the hayfield, the
dogs nipping at his heels, Snowball too, was running.

Running as only a pig could.

Squealing, barking, moo-ing, clucking, baa-ing, neighing,
squeaking, quacking. Misremembered histories. Misdirected
rages. Half-lies. Lies. Accusations. Counteraccusations. Names,
dates, places. Enemies were trampled—allies, valorized. Terror
and thrill. Round and round—all ran. All raced.

What future?

And then Snowball, that old Yorkshire boar, lost his hoofing,
slipped, and rolled down the grassy knoll into a deep ditch.
And as he lay unmoving, the shepherds jumped in after him—

their lips retracting over their teeth, and their whole snouts pushing into the lightly furred flesh of his abdomen. And deeper—into his liver, his lungs, and his heart.

When the dogs shook their faces and fur—Snowball was everywhere. And the animals looked on, in horror, as blood spattered the farm—and Minimus allowed his dogs to devour their quarry.

They'd gone hog-wild.

Some looked away. Some looked on. Always the cries of joy. Always the cries of dismay. A pig handed out tall glasses of whiskey. Even the young drank. Their cries for peace turned drunken.

What now?

A wave of hopelessness and despondency washed over the fearful creatures. What now? Everyone had so liked their new cement stalls. More of the youth called out for peace—a few of their elders, partly afraid for them, partly disgusted by them, were meting out swats for good measure. All, lean and bony with fear, cowered with an uncomprehending anxiety as they watched the inflation of the oldest and fattest and most Napoleonic dogs and pigs. ("And, uh, who's Napoleon again?" asked a nervous field mouse.)

Two more whiskey barrels were rolled out. The scene, especially among the younger animals, grew debauched. Their cries for peace became slurred and confused—unintelligible. Others shrank and pointed their forefeet.

"It's your fault!"

"No, yours!"

And in a moment, a million dreams had fallen. Be they selfish or altruistic—clink, clink, clink—they tipped like dominoes.

But then an odd thing began to happen. The attack dogs— they started to cough, and to sputter the blood that they had been drinking from their disboweled prey. They began to clutch their necks and stomachs. And they moaned and yowled, their own flesh burning.

And in the animals, the dream was reborn—but now more selfish, and more altruistic. And, with a welling-up of optimism, they watched the shepherds choke on their own prey.

They watched the shepherds fall—and writhe.

And the expression of glee worn by Minimus transformed to one of dread, as his guards dropped one by one. Killers, only a moment before, were now too helpless to lift themselves to their own feet. Yes, Minimus looked around—now he was helpless, too.

And then Snowball rose from the arena of blood—rose through the corpse—rose through the flesh that hung from the jowls of the failing shepherds. It had all been a ruse! That eaten pig wasn't Snowball! It was a poisoned side of pork!

And those dogs—they were dead dogs now!

And Snowball was alive!

Snowball was alive!

The animals had all seen him die, but there he was, alive—and now, even those who had hated him loved him.

Snowball, the cheater of death, was alive!

Snowball, the dreamer of dreams, was alive!

Yes, alive!

Snowball and the dream!

The breeze picked up, shifted sharply, and standing atop the carnage, high above the animals of the farm, Snowball's ears fluttered in the bluster! And on the current of air—the animals smelled death, and victory! And Snowball's dogs salivated—for they knew they would soon roll in it.

And thus—so too did Minimus finally understand. There was no stopping this Snowball. This avalanche.

But who, wondered Minimus, had forewarned Snowball?

And then, in the brief instant that Minimus looked from Snowball to Brutus to Pinkeye, the old pig knew all.

Brutus and Pinkeye—his closest allies, so he had thought—they were giving him up to Snowball.

Minimus looked to his chief dog—*is it true?*

Yes, Brutus lowered his head in disclosure. *Yes*, he had turned on his Prize Pig.

Yes, Brutus lowered his head, he had struggled with the question—what is loyalty? And he had decided, his loyalty was to the farm animals, as best as he could understand it. And as best he could understand it, their loyalty was to riches—their loyalty was to might. Their loyalty was to the conqueror and his gold. That was the future.

And so Minimus finally understood—Brutus had decided.

Snowball was the master of the farm, the master of the farm animals, and the master of the dogs.

And Minimus's pig's eyes sagged, the sequence of his expressions as if to say—

You, Pinkeye, even if I didn't expect it, I understand—as you saw that your destiny lay with him. And you, Brutus—of course I should have known that your allegiance would rest upon the strongest haunches. But you were my faithful dog, and I never would have known—and I would rather have died than known.

In a gesture of infinite forgiveness, and infinite anguish, Minimus extended his hoof to his former shepherd—

"Et tu, Bruté?"

And as Minimus looked into the gray eyes of his own monster, Snowball gave a haughty nod, and with an evil chuckle, the order—

"Jugular!"

And with that, whatever it meant, Minimus was set upon, and consumed by his own shepherds.

Once so strong, Minimus died gurgling and pitiable.

And all the animals saw the brightness of the future that Snowball had brought to them. And blinded by that whiteness, they hailed it.

"Snowball! Snowball! Snowball!"

And Minimus, right under their snouts, passed from this life, taking an era with him, and thinking, not of the pain in his limbs, not of the pain in his loins, but of how, maybe, it could have all been so different. The whisper of his final couplet went unheard—

To Animal Farm I forever impart,
The red, red ripe of my loyal heart.

The following Sunday Meeting, Pinkeye, in his inaugural address as the now and future and probably forever Prize Pig, assured all the populace that nothing like this would ever happen again, and that the pigs and dogs were entirely on top of things, and that nobody should worry their pretty little heads.

And that was definitely a relief, as everybody thought they had a pretty little head, and nobody liked to worry.

It was Pinkeye's solemn promise that nothing would change—and that if there should be any change, it would be for the better.

The carnival would still be built—and it would be built at top speed. All the pigs were unified in their thinking—and certainly, there was no nefarious, self-destructive specter of gluttony. No, quite the opposite, pigs were known to be a generous and equitable species. And to suppose that any pig was motivated, for example, by wealth or power, was, frankly, beyond sanity.

A pig would never intentionally undermine another pig. A pig would never intentionally deceive or prevaricate—and a pig would never set out to accomplish any goal without anything but the well-being of Animal Farm at heart. (And this well-being was not just in the hearts of the public servant pigs, who everyone knew were beyond reproach, but all the pigs—be they leaders of policy, industry, or coming attractions.) True, conceded Pinkeye, there would be "bumps," but never resulting from greed, or revenge, or political manipulations—no, not these. Rather, the exposure of any such "bump" (be it by a specially appointed prosecutor, or one of the *Trotter's* many trusty reporters) would always be excited by the integrity, and the intention of maintaining the integrity of the farm—and the initial cause of any such bump would always be discovered to be a misdirected impulse, loyalty, or subcommittee. Nobody at the top was ever really at fault—though there were often a few rotten apples at the bottom of the barrel. Or, rather, the bottom of the bottom of the barrel. Or, rather, the bottom of the bottom of the bottom of the barrel. . . .

So, speaking of bad apples—what happened to those animals involved in the disboweling attempt?

Well, as was uncovered in *Trotter*, the lone conspirator was an orangish badger by the name of Cotswold.

Dispelling groundless rumors—Minimus was unequivocally cleared of any wrongdoing. And no, nobody had seen the shepherds attack Minimus, and no, he had not been reduced to dogmeat. Rather, the dogs were as restrained and obedient as ever, and Minimus, wanting to spend more time with his piglets, had retired with his sow to their country estate. The only animal with a memory reliable enough to confirm any of this was Benjamin, who now spent all his spare time with Emerald and her son Kip—and who had no inclination, as he said, to be interrupted with silly questions. That aside, even he must have known that his silence was perceived as verification of the official record. (Kip was home-schooled due to an irregular heartbeat.)

An embittered functionary who dreamt of being a dog, Cotswold had proceeded entirely on his own initiative. And accordingly, as nothing could compromise the judicious processes of the farm, would Cotswold have been held accountable—had not he himself been subsequently assassinated by one of the beer-cart bulls.

The matter so nicely resolved, the episode was quickly looked on as, not a threat, but a reaffirmation of Animal Farm. It was not, after all, as if this kind of thing had ever happened before, or would ever happen again. And besides, as was so obviously in evidence, even when it did happen—well, justice was swift and inevitable.

VIII

IF, BY COTSWOLD'S failed disboweling attempt, there was any question as to Snowball's authority, that question was soon answered. Under Pinkeye's wise and free hoof, Snowball had successfully concluded his campaign to oust the Pilkingtons from Foxwood, and the Fredericks from Pinchfield. (With the proceeds from another bank loan, a second law firm had been retained to assist the first.) The victory was the most celebrated in all the history of Animal Farm. It was hammers, saws, and wire-clippers on the old fences that partitioned the three farms—and The Freedom Shuffle all night long.

One of the pigs put a phonograph into service—and the animals drank and caroused until dawn. Many of the pigs became so drunk that they disrobed and frolicked in a mud simulated from chocolate and almond paste. The pigs thus revealed in their undergarments, it was noted by one of the badgers that a good number of them had grown so fat so as to have no legs—just feet! The pigs were enormously gratified by the observation—and as happy as all the animals were in this fresh new world, it appeared the pigs were even happier! In a spontaneous honoring of farm triumph, it was decreed that all animals should have a regular portion of milk and apples. The pigs, meanwhile, were heard whispering excitedly about some foodstuffs called caviar and cognac—brain food, evidently, that was especially beneficial to a pig.

And perhaps owing to such beneficial brain food as this, the pigs were so very duty-conscious that not for a single night did they leave the two farmhouses derelict. Indeed, it was well before dawn—with the celebration still in full swing—that the first pigs harnessed the horses to cart their belongings to the abandoned residences.

At odds with this dignified duty-doing, however, was the swine rush on the good rooms—and the angry squeal of one pig against another. And no matter how out of the ordinary that behavior might be . . . well, for some inexplicable reason, an animal drinking whiskey couldn't help but think it was funny—downright hysterical—and even the dogs were inspired to dance and drink for another three hours!

But, of course, as it was explained at the Sunday Meeting, the animals had been wrong to laugh at such a serious problem. The pigs needed more space, urgently, and this was a matter that required immediate address. Soon comprehending the grave injustice suffered by the pigs, the animals approved a full remodeling of the Jones House, as well as the houses of Frederick and Pilkington. The basements would be finished, and rooms, toilets, and kitchens would be added. As the swine had troubling "hoofing it" (no legs, just feet), it was also deemed necessary to budget a motor vehicle for every pig— that he or she might drive from one farmhouse to another. (The distances, respectively, were two and three miles—not, as had been previously thought, 1/3 of a mile, and 1/2 of a mile. The Frederick and Pinchfield House only appeared nearby, due to something called an "optical illusion.") Also, six Japanese dogs (Shih-tzus) trained in the art of massage (shiatsu) were taken on to help the pigs relieve any stress that they might be suffering as a result of the relocation—two dogs for each house.

As Prize Pig, Pinkeye took over the master wing of the Pink House—that is, the Jones House, which, fully renovated, had been renamed. (Nobody knew where Snowball took up residence, but it was rumored to be even better than the Pink House, which was itself rather regal.) The various other pigs were assigned to their various other refurbished accommodations and offices—though none of the animals could quite decipher who was elected versus who was appointed versus who was a private citizen, or when who was elected, appointed or privatized, or for how long. But no matter, the services of the pigs meant everything to the fair. And lucky thing, the pigs seemed to be everywhere on it—occupying not only the Pink House, but the Rose House (formerly the Frederick House), and the Salmon House (formerly the Pilkington House), and at least two dozen other sundry shacks and barns that had been redesigned, redesignated, or simply reclaimed in the name of efficiency.

Lastly, before the contractors and subcontractors went on their merry ways, three huts were built, which at first were believed to be smokehouses, but were later identified as something called "saunas." They were assumed to be some sort of outdoor showers, and the animals appreciated the great sacrifice of the pigs—in that they did not have indoor showers, as did the other animals on Animal Farm. But a few of the animals were not so convinced that the saunas were outdoor showers. They thought the saunas must be an odder business, as, in winter, the pigs were seen just outside the saunas, rolling around in the snow—without their towels. Also, the humans called "investors" participated in this activity. Something agreeable only to the pink-skinned, no doubt.

Still, the pigs were happy, as after their tours and "saunas" (whatever those were) the human "investors" (whatever those were) were unusually contented. And if it was true, as it was supposed, that the investors had something to do with financing Animal Fair, there was every reason to be contented—because the construction was coming along well. Exceedingly well.

With all the new tools fashioned by the goats, the *Daily Trotter* assessed that a summer opening date was not an unreasonable expectation. To meet this objective, the only compromise that had to be made was in safety procedures— and consequently, two dogs and a duck were killed in a cement mixing accident. Well, actually, as the *Trotter* later clarified, the safety procedures hadn't really been compromised —as the accident couldn't have been foreseen, not even by a goat. Who could ever have known that the rooster driving the cement truck couldn't see over the dashboard?

Occasionally, a cow, or badger, or some sophisticated goose was overheard saying that Minimus's exit hadn't been an altogether good thing, that he had served as a kind of coagulant to the bloodstream of Animal Farm—and that without him, the farm was bleeding to death. Not many understood this argument literally—too many big words and confusing concepts—but they understood the basic idea. Things did seem to be moving a tad fast.

Maybe, suggested a few of the animals, this would be a good time to think about some of the suffering of animals in "the village out there." They obviously could use the help—a few of the rats and pigeons were even telling stories of village animals who were starving to death. . . .

After a brief interruption of hot water, apparently caused by several rats and pigeons who were nesting in the generator (they were put on sewer duty), the animals-of-the-village concerns were allayed by the *Daily Trotter*. A four-week cycle of scholarly articles led one to conclude for oneself (whether one read the series in totem, or in part, or even just perused the pictures) that in a village market, the best thing the animals of Animal Farm could possibly do for the village economy was worry about themselves. They'd do what they did best, while others did what they did best. And they'd all share. And that, even the most skeptical of the animals agreed, was a sound argument.

Live good—for the good of the village.

So, for several months, in a frame of mind that prided itself on a long hard day's work, and sighed to itself with a long hot shower after that long hard day, the carnival progressed. And pleasantly enough.

"We're all in this together," Snowball would say.

And yet . . . that spring, just as the flowers blossoms and the sun spoke of coming dewberries, the animals faced a heartbreaking episode—a more heartbreaking episode, nobody could recall.

One of the rats, an old English rat who worked for the pigs, reported that he had uncovered the traitor who had passed the blueprints of the Twin Mills to Mr. Frederick of the Pinchfield Farm. It was at the first Meeting in May, that fateful Sunday, that the accusations were leveled at Filmont the Labrador.

Brutus, who remained Top Dog under Pinkeye, laid out the irrefutable evidence that had been brought to him by the rat. But even so, the animals held their breath and uttered prayers to themselves—as they still fostered a hope that Filmont could explain the charge away. Filmont—whom the animals loved above all others! Filmont—who, no matter how far an animal could recite the alphabet, loved that animal back!

How could Filmont be guilty of such a betrayal?

But Filmont, faced by Brutus, had no tale of explanation. The slumping Labrador offered no resistance to the allegations as they were brought against him. Yes, he confessed, it was exactly that way. He had stolen the blueprints during the course of a follow-up examination in the laboratory of Thomas the goat—and then he had given them over. He had been desperate to free his love, Sandra-Marjorie the collie, from Mr. Pilkington. And upon hearing that Mr. Frederick was prepared to allow Bilby Pilkington to drown the puppies (the boy relished such tasks), the Labrador had seen no option but to make a deal with his former owner—a man who had nearly kicked him to death.

Filmont had always been a motivator—an animal that made labor go more easily. Moreover, he had been a facilitator in this labor of living—and the animals felt deeply betrayed. How could he have passed such "classified" material to the enemy? ("Classified," a word new to most of the farm, was nevertheless a word that was being bandied around not a little in connection with this treachery.) Mr. Frederick was a man who liked cockfights—a man with a belly swelling with the meat of cow, sheep, pig, goat, and bird. And he was no man to be trusted with such sensitive information as the plans for the Twin Mills. Filmont's arguments that he hadn't wanted to hurt anyone—that he had thought Mr. Frederick merely wanted to build a windmill of his own—were met with muzzles twisted in scorn and hatred.

Pinkeye immediately announced that all the pigs were in agreement—the Labrador would be drawn and quartered by the horses. This statement, however, was subsequently retracted. And two days later, at the Sunday State of the Farm Address, Snowball put forth a revised argument. (Someone asked if Sunday wasn't supposed to be the day of the Meeting, but they were quickly silenced by a shepherd, as this was not the time for discussion.) Snowball argued that death was too good—that Filmont should be forced to live on as some kind of example. Perhaps he should be made an exhibit of the carnival—and spend his days on display, confessing his betrayal time and time again.

During the week, as the pigs and goats deliberated upon the fate of the Labrador, it was discovered that, despite Filmont's agreement with the humans, in the days just prior to their eviction from Foxwood and Pinchfield, Bilby Pilkington had been permitted to drown Filmont's puppies anyway—just because he wanted to. It was further revealed that Sandra-Marjorie the collie, mourning her whelps, had gone mad, and bitten Bilby on the cheek as he taunted her. Immediately thereafter, she had been led to the quarry and put down. Bilby had been allowed to employ his crossbow. Alongside the burlap sack of dead puppies, the bloodhounds found her there . . . in the standing water. The assumption was that Bilby had made the Animal Farm quarry his place of execution to ensure that Filmont the Labrador should find out what end had befallen his family.

And Filmont did find out.

Apprised of his collie and puppies on Friday, the Labrador was found dead in his stall on Saturday. He had been under the constant vigilance of three shepherds, so nobody knew how he had gotten the box of chocolates (fatal to canines). They only knew that in the morning he was dead, the box was empty, and the note he left behind spoke of his greatest sorrow—that he had never managed to dig under that fence, to see his collie Sandra-Marjorie one last time.

After Filmont's death, it was realized that the dogs had never managed to establish how Filmont had been communicating with Mr. Frederick. By rat, by bird? Who was the courier? For weeks, there was talk of demoting the three bloodhound inter-rogators, who had failed to ask Filmont these crucial questions, to sheepdogs. But when it was realized that they had wanted to ask the questions, but had been thwarted by something called "animal rights"—well, those, as one might say, were thrown to the wolves.

As security was now an issue, just as the dogs, more than ever, followed orders from the pigs, so too, more than ever, did the animals follow orders from the dogs.

And what demanding work it was to maintain order! The dogs needed six meals a day just to sustain themselves! And a dog on six meals a day—that was a formidable beast! A beast that commanded attention—sort of a rude, not-too-quick pig, with fur.

And the carnival?

Yes, overwrought. Yes, overbudget. And yes, in spite of everything, on schedule—to be opened by summer's end. Already, fifteen tradeshow shacks and the Ferris Wheel (which would be one of the main attractions of the park) were completed. In preparation for vending and ticket sales, the animals had been enrolled in a new class, "Money, paper and coin." Students were instructed on denominations, addition and subtraction, and the sniff-test—which allowed even animals with the most rudimentary intelligence to identify counterfeit currency. All the animals, including those who had never been able to visually identify a genuine note from a fraudulent one, were easily able to master the olfactory method.

As opening night approached, pigeons were sent out into the village—to paint signs and billboards, to mount placards and banners, and to just generally coo and warble of the wonder of Animal Fair.

I'll go to the Animal Fair—cast off my daily cares.
I'll stuff my face with more than my share.
And drink 'till I dance with the bear.

The carnival gates were thrown wide on Midsummer's night—the anniversary of the rebellion. The new flag was raised, an old rifle was fired from the foot of the flagstaff— and then, a tremendous neon sign was illuminated. For the first time ever, the blazing pink and green proclaimed—

ANIMAL FAIR

With this, Snowball announced from his soapbox that Animal Fair was open for business. Turnstiles turned. Electric lights were switched on—and in a unification of every dream of every animal everywhere, the night was turned to day. None could deny the power of the spectacle—thousands of lights burned the sky!

The very stars were dimmed by the magnificence of Animal Fair!

And the first night of the park's operation was a night of fulfillment and gain. There were visitors enough—and they lined up to eat the food, play the games, and ride the rides. The Ferris Wheel was especially popular. Couples would embrace and look across the stream and the road—to the village. And then, depending on their species, they would knead each other's withers, or rub bills, or mash lips.

True, towards the middle of the evening, about ten o'clock, there was a slight problem with the crepe stand, when it caught fire and collapsed. But, thanks to the prudent planning of the goats, the tradeshow shack was on the periphery of the park, and not neighbored closely by any other concessions. The dogs managed the situation capably enough, and the evening, yet young, had ample time to recover. By midnight, some of the pigs were even claiming that the fire intentionally staged—a diversion from expectation. There had been something marvelous about it, they argued—and the animals couldn't disagree with that, as, to watch a building burning, well . . . even if it was a little frightening, it was a marvel. And, as the pigs reminded them, nobody had been hurt.

The fireworks display at closing time was the most spectacular anyone had ever seen. Few among those present had ever seen a fireworks display before, but even so, all agreed, this display, as far as fireworks displays went, must have ranked awfully high. There was a small, accidental conflagration on the dock in the pond, but again, to the hoots of spectators, it was attended, in good order, by the dogs. (Coincidentally, several of the wharf rats who worked the docks were reported missing. Interviews were made, leads were pursued, and the rats were found. They were quite safely lodged downstream, it was reported in the *Trotter*, where they had taken up permanent residence.)

With the closing of the park, it went around that the evening had been so lucrative that the pigs predicted the bank loans would be paid off earlier than had been projected. This, in consequence, would somehow save the fair a good deal of money in something called "interest." ("Well," joked a goose, "I think it's more confusing than interesting!") Regardless, all enjoyed the after-hours festivities, and every animal was apportioned a pint of beer—and where each pig would customarily receive a pint, tonight, each pig received a half-gallon. All toasted to the pigs—and their powerful thirst! (The goats, not interested in beer, drank something called "martinis.")

And ahhhh, what a wonderful night!

And ahhhh, the splendors of the chicken fight! And the bliss of a dog-tired stupor!

The scamper of pigs' feet carried forth from the Jones House until 10 AM the next morning, when the park reopened. Food delivery services had been arriving at a rate of four an hour since one o'clock the night before. The ducks, who cleaned house for the pigs, reported a scene that included fifteen pigs sleeping in a hot tub full of tapioca pudding, and two pigs still battling it out in a test-of-the-wills chip-eating challenge. (It was definitely not, the pigs would later insist, dispelling an unsubstantiated rumor, a pork-rind challenge.) At noon, the last delivery boy arrived, with two gallons of guacamole. Only Emerald the counting donkey could give any adequate account of what guacamole was. Few of the animals had ever heard of an avocado.

Notwithstanding the animals' lack of familiarity with the green fruit, or vegetable, with a large pit, they had been introduced to an unimaginable variety of food—a variety of such magnitude that it would have once been thought impossible. Besides the fried bananas and cheese fries, there were candy-covered apples, red-hot fireballs, and numerous other delectables, such as chocolate-coated crickets, ants, and dung beetles.

For weeks, it was privately debated among the pigs and goats whether or not Animal Fair should serve meat goods. And in the end, after a struggle of conscience, which all the animals deeply appreciated, Snowball announced the compromise that had been made.

It would be permissible to sell beef, pork, mutton, goat, and fowl, as long as the flesh was not obtained from Animal Fair cows, pigs, sheep, goats, or birds. Furthermore, in keeping with the principles of Animal Fair, even if the park animals did sell meat products, they would not be allowed to eat it themselves (although the pigs noted with good humor that preventing one or two of the dogs from getting into it, on occasion, might prove an impossibility). Any meat product, stressed the pigs, would only come from the butcher—and never from the fair.

In the hard years of the past, the butcher had helped the fair by purchasing the hides and flesh of patriots, who at the time of their natural deaths had chosen to make, entirely voluntarily, that ultimate sacrifice. (Of course, this act of dedication was deemed no longer required, and the butcher would, henceforth, merely act as an undertaker, and surgeon, to the Animal Fair animals.) And after several minutes of the sheep shouting, "The butcher, only from the butcher!" the pigs further amended that no juvenile animals would be served—nor would any item be served that had been obtained through the torture or discomfort of an animal. (The butcher had agreed to provide meat derived solely from animals, not-from-Animal-Fair animals, who had died of natural causes—such as old age, illness, or unavoidable accident.) There would be no baby back ribs, said the pigs—and no veal, or pullets, or "foie gras."

And here, an odd thing happened, as despite the fact that none of the other animals, except perhaps the goats, knew what foie gras was, the pigs repeatedly stressed that foie gras had been disallowed. In a display wholly uncharacteristic of the porcine disposition (actually, the display was far more characteristic of the sheep, who, unlike the pigs, were not known for their gray matter), they chanted "foie gras" for close to five minutes—during which time they watered, mightily, at the mouth. In the days after this odd demonstration, it required the *Daily Trotter* to explain to the animals that the mention of foie gras, whatever it was, had not thrown the pigs into a frenzy, and that they had not been salivating for appetite, but for a dedication to Animal Fair, and the rules that would govern it.

And with every day the park was open (and it was *every* day —their noble enterprise, and, in the process, to learn not only about themselves, but about all the other species that visited the park. Animal Fair welcomed all animals—the humans, as they were also animals, being heartily included in this invitation. Furless, perhaps, tailless, perhaps—but animals nevertheless.

Surprisingly enough, the humans were wholly enthusiastic about this inclusion. One of the most popular exhibits, indeed, was one that had originally been conceived as educational. Throughout the entire outlying area, the voices of men and women could always be heard emanating outwards from the "Animalism" tent.

> *"How d'you do Mr. Gnu?" I said to a gnu I knew.*
> *And to you, you adoraboo ewe, and lovaboo Miss Emu, I doffed*
>   *my caparoo.*
> *And I waved to the shrews and the caribous riding bicycles built*
>   *for two.*
> *And a cow went "Moo,' and a cat went "Mew."*
> *And I said, "Toodle-doo, Mr. Kangaroo." For I am*
>   *an animal, too!*

The humans—they sang the song of the animals, and they hurrahed. The animals had overcome the tyrant! They had cast off their chains! They were free! Free!

It was everybody's dream!

Another exhibit that drew an unexpectedly large crowd was that of Martha-Lo the merry-go-round Pony, who was actually a second-generation Animal Fair animal—although she was so other worldly it was hard to imagine she originated from anywhere. *Canary*, a new magazine that focused on topical events in the village and on the fairgrounds, published a lovely biographical sketch of the "headliner." Her raking-the-hay cover was quite controversial.

Martha-Lo was a bay pony with sunny highlights, who, though many of the other animals couldn't see it, managed to convince a large proportion of the visitors to the park that she had "that certain something." For the talent element of her performance, she recited the alphabet to the letter I, and handed out home-baked cookies. A few of her personal weasels resented her, in that without a glass of fresh-pressed beet juice and two sugar cubes to top off the hour, the show could not go on.

And there were other acts, too, that had their share of success —headliners such as Kissilvis the dancing bear, Brandovitz the unforgetting, unforgettable elephant, and Kokia Bobcat, who was awesome and sensual.

But over the coming months, many of the acts, which had risen to popularity, subsequently, fell in popularity—and so reduced, these acts, as they had come, went. And as hard as it was to say good-bye, it was realized that this was the natural course of acts in an amusement park. After an audience was exhausted by a given spectacle, it was only to be expected that the spectacle would move on to another venue—preferably, a far-away venue, as nobody, not even the performers themselves, liked to remember an old act. And as for losing friends, the animals learned to make new friends—though it must be said, there was something a little lonely about having to explain one's life all over again. So much so that, after a while, most animals didn't bother anymore.

It was not, after all, a personal matter, but a professional matter. And more than anything else, it was the enormous ambition of such an undertaking as the park that made its impression on the animals. And it was as a result of this impression (Ambition! Ambition! Ambition!) mingled with the experience of these seemingly countless entertainers (whose itinerant life was hugely romantic) that a staggeringly high number of the park animals began to dimly suspect, and forthwith to discover (hooray!) that they had talents of their own. (Besides, with no friends around, why not travel?) Regular auditions were initiated by the pigs, and though very few of the animals were ever bestowed a tent of their own, there was the rare exception. A badger named Otto was given top billing by the *Trotter*. The headliner's "I eat worms, dirt, and rocks" stall was a favorite of pig and critic alike.

Some animals were so determined to raise their small talents to a point of headlining that, out of their own earnings, they hired pigs to become their trainers. And thus, it was at the urging of the animals themselves that many a boar strapped his whip back on.

There were other changes—most noticeably, a pit was dug out of the old pastureland, and the daily mounds of garbage were pitched into it. When it was filled to the top, the mass was burned down. The septic waste, from the outhouses available to the visitors of the park, was also added to this stew. Despite the grumblings of some of the animals, it was proven by the goats that this disposal system had nothing to do with the ground-water problem. After two dead beavers were discovered in the pond (they had floated down from the Woodlands) and two chickens died from their daily glasses of reconstituted pineapple juice, the goats announced that a water tank was being brought in, and that from now on water would be purchased from a natural spring—and that the well water should not be used for anything but cleaning and bathing.

Having extended its borders, Animal Fair had to contend with the two new neighboring farms (to the east and, respectively, the west) of Haberdash and Dilldiddle. And it was soon discovered, by the tireless bloodhounds, that these new neighbors had been responsible for the contamination of the ground water. And while the contamination was inconvenient, the pigs were secure in their conviction that they could employ the situation to their own advantage in a pending lawsuit against the two enemies. (Luckily, the pigs had retained their lawyers from their previous lawsuit against their previous enemies.) It was hoped, with some good reason for hope, that these evil, wasteful regimes (these new evil, wasteful regimes) would soon be toppled. It was not long before many of the animals had entirely forgotten there had ever been a Foxwood or Pinchfield, and the age-old lawsuit was assumed to have always been against Haberdash and Dilldiddle. It was their defeat that would bring Animal Fair's ultimate victory (as victorious as Animal Fair was already).

So, with this object in mind (more victory!) the animals worked hard, and the pigs and goats encouraged them to work even harder—it was a war of work, said Snowball. And moreover, hard work satisfied the individual objectives of many of the animals, who looked forward to better days for themselves—days when they wouldn't have to work so hard.

And to the enormous satisfaction of the pigs, the bank loans were paid off early. And everyone knew that was good for the fair, whyever that might be. And the pigs, who had made friends with the bankers (they drank whiskey with banking "executives" on a regular basis, in a dedicated effort to keep up good relations), took out new loans, which was also excellent for the fair, whyever that might be. . . .

And things were going well—so well, actually, that it was suggested in the *Daily Trotter* that there was too much hard work, and too much ambition. The animals, who were all working seven days a week, were collecting far too much in wages, and were therefore driving up something called "inflation." This meant, said the *Trotter*, that it was time for the animals to work less hard, and to have more ambitions about flying kites and playing croquet—and fewer about sequined mangers and pearl-studded bow ties. A new three-day work-week was legislated. But because the kite field and croquet course were closed to all but pigs and goats (only the pigs and goats could afford the prohibitive "member fee") the animals were unable to fly kites, and play croquet, as had been suggested. A few of the animals took up something called "dice," but mostly, the animals just stared out their windows for the four days a week they weren't working.

And at first, as the fair animals were due for a little relaxation, that wasn't so bad. Actually, it was terrific—even the voles said so. But after a few weeks, when everyone had rested up, it got to be a bore, and the animals spent the days they weren't working looking forward to the days they were working. It was soon amended that an animal was permitted to work more than three days a week—but anything over three days would be considered entirely voluntary, and would warrant no extra benefits—food or otherwise. And without extra food to sustain extra work, most animals deemed such exertion gratuitous. They'd rather just look out their windows, and if they couldn't actually fly a kite or play a round of croquet, just think about flying a kite or playing a round of croquet. Some held that the answer was beer, or if they could afford it, whiskey—both beverages being available in the park.

A few of the more ambitious animals, who were hoping to demonstrate themselves deserving of some managerial post, might take on an extra day here and there. But even they would tire of it. The best thing that could be said of the three-day workweek was that it allowed several fair animals to get fat—and that was, in a sense, a victory, as aside from the pigs, dogs and goats, there had not been a fat animal on the fairgrounds that anyone, not even Benjamin, could remember. And if you got fat, the three-day workweek wasn't so bad anymore, as fat animals didn't like to move much anyway.

The most major drawback of the three-day workweek was that the managerial positions, which had been coming fast and furious for some time, seemed suddenly . . . well, infrequent. It was as if, wedged behind their counters, everyone was stuck in one place. This misconception, however, was soon put to rest by *Canary*. Time and again, *Canary* recounted the stories behind the appointments—always a triumph over adversity. And the animals liked to hear that, because for all the good things about their lives, as they sat in front of their windows those four days a week, somehow, their lives did seem adverse—though by all means they did love Animal Fair, and did appreciate it as the best place around for an animal, which it really was.

It might be supposed that all those long hours at the window thinking about Martha-Lo the Pony bred humiliation and envy. But as a science article in the *Trotter* had linked bitterness and resentment to failure, and failure to ongoing failure, few found that they themselves were anything but optimistic. (And also, maybe, a little tipsy from one of those martinis!)

Yes, perhaps on occasion tempers ran a little short. And yes, perhaps, there was that new pesky problem of the "criminanimals." But, most assuredly, none of trouble resulted from anything akin to feelings of stagnation and aspiration unfulfilled. No siree, how could life be anything but a wonder, when one had a window?

Now collecting salaries, the animals were also paying bills—food, water, lodging, utilities, and taxes (taxation, the most difficult concept to grasp, took up 1/3 to 1/2 of each class in the "Wage Earner" seminar). So, fortunately, as for the robberies and hold-ups, there was not really all that much to take.

This, combined with the fact that the crimes tended to be a

bit on the silly side, let few of the animals, and certainly none of the pigs or the goats, take the problem too seriously. They had all seen crimes before—real crimes like Cotswold's disboweling attempt, and Filmont's betrayal of the dream. And as far as a couple of porcupines bungling the burglary of a jalapeno grasshopper stand, or the outrageous behavior of a sheep, a chicken, and a horse in a love triangle—it was laughable. Lowlife like that couldn't recite the alphabet to the letter E.

Still, some discipline was called for, and any animal guilty of a crime was sentenced to perform in a sideshow. (Some animals actually seemed to commit crimes for the sole reason that they had no other recourse than becoming sideshow performers.) In the "Criminals of the Courtyard" exhibit, the guilty animal would confess his or her crime eighteen times a day (thrice an hour for six hours) while wearing no clothing at all, aside from a yellow hat with a bell at the top. The exhibit grew so popular, and profitable, that many held crime was not a problem at all—but merely a source for the sideshow. The pigs and dogs were unanimous on this point—the sins of a few depraved common frogs and pygmy shrews inspired more mirth than panic. A domestic squabble between a jack-hare and his doe? The torrid affair of a smooth newt and a warty newt, or a field mouse and a house mouse? A shoplifting goldfinch?!

Honestly, crimes like that—it was all too amusing!

But in the months to come, the crime got worse.

Probably, it was partly due to this, in addition to the water-supply problem and the poor air quality (the garbage fires, every other day, lingered over the grounds in the form of a black cloud) that a large number of the animals began to leave the fair—deciding, perhaps, that it was time for a new start in the suburbs. (The pigs and goats, having bought up the countryside, were building housing developments.) Besides, the life of the fair animals, be they entertainers or just "carneys," was a wandering, cast-your-bread-on-the-waters kind of life—and in a life like that, an urge to move on just had to be honored.

On the flip side, Animal Fair offered enormous opportunity, and there were always plenty of new animals coming in. (Everyone, from the original farm animals to the old-time newcomers, got in on the dumbcomer jokes—it was commonly suggested that flushing the punch bowl was a good way to ruin a dumbcomer party.) And the toxic water and brown air? Well, as the pigs said, that was a boon of crucial vitamins and minerals, and a terrific invigorant to the system.

"Ahhh," sighed the pigs, who never left the fair, once they arrived, "breathe that rich dark air! Like good soil! I'll tell you, nothing's better! That's the sweet smell of success!"

That notwithstanding, more and more of the original farm animals, coughing, departed. And then, more and more of the animals who replaced those original farm animals, also coughing, also departed. And so gradually, of Animal Fair, it could no longer be said that there was a local community.

But there was, as the pigs liked to put it, a village community.

From all over the village, animals came to try out their dreams. Daily, they came, sure that they had something to offer. And as difficult as it was to succeed (even in a free land like Animal Fair), every wave of immigrants arrived with the self-assurance that they were better—and could raise themselves from menial labor with greater ease and poise than had any immigrants preceding them. And in a carnival atmosphere, which thrived upon new blood, new energy, and the occasional new idea, there was nothing wrong with a little confidence. "Be independent," the pigs would say to the newcomers in the orientation classes—

"You're one of us, now."

There were still, of course, familiar faces—Benjamin, Emerald, Kip, Temescula, and all the pigs and dogs. But even of these, many chose to work on the fairgrounds while making their homes elsewhere. A new subgroup of animals was created, called "commuters." Hobart the bull joined this subclass, purchasing an old dairy barn just down the road. Having taken out a bank loan of his own, Hobart and his family moved their ice-cream parlor to the dairy barn, the renovation of which Hobart completed, after much labor, with his young brother, Goober. Applying the lessons of the fair to the village, their business was extraordinarily successful.

Indeed, the lesson of Animal Fair promised such extraordinary success that it seemed all the village was joining the carnival!

And yet, on the fairgrounds, the crime got worse.

Considerably worse.

It was after the Jones House itself had suffered a break-in and two assaults that an announcement was made at one of the now sparsely attended Sunday Addresses.

The goats (in all their wisdom), at the behest of the pigs (in all their benevolence), had added two new Commandments. (There'd been some talk of making the restrictions upon meat-eating into Commandments, and this issue, it was also announced by the pigs, had been resolved to everyone's satisfaction. After careful study, the subject would henceforth be officially deemed not-quite-significant-enough to merit a Commandment. Honestly, if someone ate a shrimp now and again . . . well, why bother? So what if they ate a shrimp? Or a lobster? Or a pheasant stuffed with raisins and apricots?)

On the tar wall, beside the poem, *All Animals Eat Pie*, the two new Commandments had been painted under the pre-existing commandment. Together, the Three Commandments read—

1. *It's entirely up to you.*
2. *But you better not steal.*
3. *And you better not hurt anyone.*

These were excellent additions, undoubtedly—though in practice they seemed to mean that there was not much recreation to be had, anymore. The dogs, on constant patrol, were trained to respond to anything even remotely suspicious. And just hoofing-it around the park on a moonlit night seemed suspicious enough to the dogs. It ran contrary to reason— why would animals be wandering around, when they could be in their own stall, sitting in front of their own windows? (And nobody wanted trouble with the dogs, as conditions in the Criminals of the Courtyard exhibit had become, in every respect, objectionable.)

And where once, in such a circumstance, the youth might have offered reprieve, now, they offered none—as they'd all been sent off to school. And even of those who'd come back (many didn't), nobody had the faintest notion what to say to them. (The youth, likewise, had no idea what to say to their parents.) One of the geese accidentally called her gosling, who had grown into a tall, egotistical gander, "a brainwashed stranger," though she later claimed she had meant to say, "a well-polished ranger." Mostly, the youngsters wanted to be left to their own devices, "to do their own thing," which, by the estimation their parents, seemed to be breaking the two new Commandments. (You better not steal. You better not hurt anyone.) And no matter how many times, for example, the pullets were told there couldn't be 200 dancing chickens at one fair, every one of them was sure that she would be the one, even if there were only one. Unhappily, the truth was that there hadn't once been a headlining dancing chicken. (Neither, a tic-tac-toe chicken.) Young beasts, recently graduated from the village schools, loafed in their parents' stalls and did nothing (usually in groups), convincing themselves that they would magically be appointed to positions of power—as this was a chance which, once given, they could surely manage. After all, if Temescula the chicken could do it . . . well then! Their parents must have been real idiots to have been outwitted by Temescula. It was something of a disgrace to be sired by the likes of shopkeepers and laborers—even if they were, over-all, fairly satiated shopkeepers and laborers.

To be blunt, the youths identified with anyone but their comfortable and not-so-distinguished parents. What was to admire? They were not rebels, and not emperors.

Still, everyone was comfortable—the stalls were lighted and air-conditioned, and the windows were clean and large, and the young would be young. And obviously, this was heaven on Earth (or the closest thing to heaven there was on Earth), and the parents wanted their young to be entertainers, too. Entertainers or leaders. And they loved and admired their mysterious, educated brood. And they thought that maybe the youth were right—they would become entertainers, or leaders. And progressively, the age that the young were sent away was lowered—as loving parents wanted to give their progeny every possible advantage.

And this was how things were, and how they stayed.

And stayed.

The following May, an announcement was made that Snowball would deliver a special speech at the Sunday Address. Pinkeye usually attended to such formalities—and through the week, Snowball's speech was increasingly antici-pated, as by Saturday (like every other Saturday), the animals had spent three days sitting in front of their cash registers in their tradeshow stands (peanuts, hot corn, ice cream, hot dogs) and three days staring out their window (drinking freshly brewed tea, and eating freshly bought cupcakes), hoping they wouldn't be held-up, beat-up, or if they did something wrong and got captured by the shepherds, sent-up. (The criminanimal sideshow was upstream.) There were so many rules and regulations to protect an animal's freedom—one just couldn't keep track of it all! *Respect the dogs. Respect the law. Respect the dogs. Respect the law.*

"Many years ago," announced Snowball, when the Sunday Address had come, "our founding fathers sowed the seeds of our society—and now we have reaped the yields. Yields of fortunes, and hopes bedazzling. They foresaw a day when animals would work a three-day week, and all animals would have heated stalls. And now, we work three-day weeks, and have not only heated stalls—but air-conditioned stalls! And electricity! And hot and cold running water, and windows, and anything else that you, as the stall owner, might have chosen!"

"What we have chosen!" bleated the sheep.

"We live the dream!" Snowball's fur-tipped ears shook with excitement—

"So now, we must dream more!"

"Dream more! More!" cried the sheep.

"The scope of what we can have is only limited by the scope of what we can want!"

Here, there were cheers and shouts all around.

"Way to tell'em Snowball!"

"That's right, Snowball!"

"Well said, Snowball!"

And Snowball was aglow—

"Ours is a good way of life! And a long way of life. No

more is our time cut short by the barbarity of veal, and baby back ribs, and other such crimes against Animality!"

"Animality!" repeated the sheep.

"And not only do we live the length of our natural lives—we live those lives surrounded by our loving families! Our young are not sold out from under us! The chickens keep their eggs! The dogs keep their pups! Yes, all of us keep our offspring—who are educated at the finest institutes in the village!"

A cry went out for the offspring. The animals were proud.

"It's true, Snowball! It's true!" shouted Fleur the cow, who was especially bursting with love for her calf, Kirwin, who had the highest test scores in his class for two semesters in a row. The address was then momentarily disturbed, however, as Fleur, who had not seen Kirwin in eight months, suddenly fell on her side, overcome with emotion. When she was righted, Snowball concluded—

"We all serve ourselves. And we all serve the village. It has finally come to pass that the prosperity of one is the prosperity of the other! We all serve—by serving ourselves!"

"Ourselves! Ourselves! Ourselves!" interjected the sheep.

Snowball raised his cloven hoof for calm—

"The rebellion has delivered a hundred-fold more than it promised! And I declare, today, that we are all victorious rebels!"

Wings flapped—hooves met hooves in applause. And even Benjamin, the only one who could possibly remember anything about the rebellion, or what it had promised, was hee-hawing with a delight nobody had ever before seen him exhibit. He ee-ored and nuzzled his companion, Emerald, and her growing son, Kip, who had become almost a son to him. Emerald was seen to be looking around the room with a joy of her own—

almost as if she were counting all the happy muzzles in the room.

Neither Benjamin nor Emerald had ever been looked to with such a warm respect—she and he and Kip, they were the happy family. And Benjamin beamed with approval—these times were better, these times were betterer, these times were the betterest ever!

And, well then, nodded the animals, if Benjamin thought that the dream had been realized, it must have been so! Benjamin always knew—and nobody could fool a donkey! And the animals stretched their mouths into that shape they had recently been assigned in their classes. The hours of practice had been long and arduous—but now, the hard work was paying off.

Every animal nodded and looked to every other animal, who was also nodding (Yes! Yes! All together!) and pulling his or her mouth and snout into that shape. A smile. They were all smiling!

IX

DESPITE SNOWBALL'S rebound, to the beavers, Filmont's Betrayal, as well as the disboweling attempt, had demonstrated the flimsy values of the Pig Fair—and an inherent vulnerability. To Diso, Snowball looked weak, and with his many pursuits, overextended. And Diso, seeing an opportunity to capitalize on this disadvantage, made a tactical reassessment. It was, after all, merely a matter of necessity that Diso had made any treaty with the Pig Fair. It had always been a compromise of the Beaver Code to make concessions to the nincompoops. And now was the time to return to that higher ideal, as it had been put forth by Moses.

It was in the cool comfort of the bunkers that the raven, slurping down one *Limax maximus* after another (evidently, this bird didn't have to wait for the Lodestar to get his 1600 slugs), spoke eloquently on the subject of returning the village to Woodlands. Ponds everywhere. Of course, as favorable a circumstance as many of the Woodlands animals (especially the beavers) thought this would represent, it was equally well established that this was a plan to which the pigs of the Pig Fair would not be disposed. And as there would be no cooperation on the part of the enemy (though the beavers couldn't imagine that once the ponds were reinstated even the pigs wouldn't be happier—as ponds really were the better way), a stratagem of intrigue was deployed.

In his bitterness, Mr. Frederick had supplied the beavers not only with the plans for the Twin Mills that he had acquired from his former Labrador, Filmont, but the plans to the Jones House, which had been passed on by a disgruntled cleaning duck. Making his last kerosene collection from the unsuspecting pigs, Diso plotted his rise to power—and the assault that would bring it about. He had, at his disposal, many loyal soldiers. Even a rabbit or a frog could become angry.

And they had.

Especially with the opening of the fences between Foxwood, Pinchfield, and the Pig Fair, many of the Woodlands animals, like the beavers, had reassessed. Droves of Woodlands creatures had crossed over to the new territories now under the auspices of the Pig Fair—and some, with even greater ambitions, had gone to the Pig Fair itself. And of those Woodlands animals who remained, there had grown an even greater determination—be it to leave, or stay behind.

Suffice it to say, whether they were steadfast dig-in-your-hoofers, or secret take-to-your-hooves-first-chance-you-getters, the Woodlands animals lived with the perpetual fear that they would die as a result of some bad policy the beavers had—in response to some bad policy the pigs had. The pigs, certainly now, possessed the resources to kill themselves a whole pile of frogs, toads, moles, rabbits, mice, rats, shrews, squirrels, and deer—all of whom were more or less peaceful vegetarians who could usually be found sitting around. Easy targets. But even if the pigs did kill a bunch of vegetarians, that wouldn't put an end to it, because they'd never get Diso, or any of the beavers. They were too well bunkered in—just as the pigs were too well protected by the dogs. (And besides, there were always more pigs and beavers.) Some of the Woodlands animals had the feeling the fair animals might also be living with the fear that the activities of their leaders would get them killed. Odd how it never got the leaders killed. It was always a rabbit or a duck (or for that matter, anything but a pig, goat, dog, or beaver) who seemed to be taking the big chances. It was always, "more risk this," "more risk that," and "more bravery blah blah blah." It seemed as if the only animals who weren't militant, and didn't want to kill anyone, were the animals who weren't in power—as well as being, coincidentally, the animals who were likely to get killed.

That is, the only ones who didn't want to commit murder might be murdered—funny, that.

From kerosene technology, the beavers had expanded their military capabilities. They had learned how to disable dynamite—whether by pulling out the wick, or dampening the gunpowder with water. Through these methods, they had collected numerous sticks of the explosive—as the farmers Frederick and Pilkington had become wholly obsessed, in their final hours, with the destruction of beaver dams. The beaver sabotage had rather riled them. And as bent as the farmers had been on the destruction of the dams—they'd eventually succeeded. But not before the beavers had amassed a sizeable pile of gunpowder—for which they were eager to find a use. And now, the old colonialists gone, the new one, the Pig Fair, was all that remained.

A pie shop had been opened in the heart of the Woodlands. Indeed, all the village was dotted with pie shops.

But Diso, too, had infiltrated the village. Student beavers abounded. (And those professorial goat types were surprisingly unsuspicious.)

And on this point of counterattack, Moses, though he would assign no specific undertaking, was unrestrained in his invoking of the Ancient Beaver Code. Killing nincompoops, as he explained it, was not actually murder (which of course was expressly prohibited by the Code), but, to the contrary, an act of heroism that would guarantee one's place on the Sugarcandy Lodestar (even if one slipped up once or twice on the pie thing). This information, added to the knowledge that dying for the Beaver Code also guaranteed a place on the Lodestar, left the beavers dizzy-headed—and they swam in the maniacal whirlpool of their own minds working out heroic scenarios.

And . . . as the beavers ploughed through their cedar chips and grandiose schemes, there was, to impel them forward, that distant pulse—that Woodlands torment that must one day be ceased.

> *I went to the animal show, where all of the animals go.*
> *Said a flea to a fly in a flue, "Oh fly, what shall I do?"*
> *Said the fly, "Let us flee!" Said the flea, "Let us fly!"*
> *So they flew through a flaw in the flue.*

Yes, the beavers assured their rabid-eyed followers (lost geese and porcupines who had found their way in beaver's fervor), beyond the fleas in the blankets, beyond the mealy bugs in the flour, beyond the termites in the toolshed, there are bigger things to come.

X

THERE WAS MONEY to spend. The animals had it—and for the first time in their lives, it seemed, a lot of it. And yet, there were also those nettlesome "bills," and many were forced to resort to another mysterious new fiscal introduction called "credit," which was understood dimly, if at all. (Every month—"rent," "water," "electricity," and, for example, those funny little pills that prevented one from keeling over, fat and dead, or those funny little bottles of magic potion that protected one from premature loss of feathers.) On the up side, however, it was nice to have booties for one's paws, and quaintly colored tail ribbons for special occasions. Several of the cows had always wanted waist-chains, and now they had them. Sexy, those, agreed the bulls. The ducks, who had long believed that the kazoo was the most melodic instrument, could now afford their own, and were often heard at their lessons. No Woodlands duck had a kazoo. (Only the voles could endow any redeeming musicality to the racket of the ducks, whom the voles saw as spiritual brothers—as, despite their affinity for honking and kazoos, the ducks, like the voles, tended to an unhurried and pacific disposition.)

Also, whiskey, beer, and martinis, were popular ways to spend one's money. Cigarettes, too, had grown, as of late, ever so fashionable.

"It's all about enjoying life," Snowball would say.

So, the newcomer animals did the laundry and changed the hay, while the old-time animals worked their three-day weeks in their heated and air-conditioned carnival shacks, and spent their four-day weekends doing, well, whatever they liked. They could smoke, drink, or dream. One might even travel, if fit enough and inclined to foray from one's stall. And even were one not so inclined, or so fit, there was always the possibility of putting in another window.

According to the *Trotter*, it was largely the annexing of the Foxwood and Pinchfield farms that allowed this higher standard of living. The lumber operation was quite lucrative, as was the strip-mining. The new quarry and toxic waste disposal sites also provided a steady income. As did the parking. Over 29% of Foxwood, and 38% of Pinchfield had been promptly paved over to supply parking for the growing number of visitors who arrived at the carnival with motor vehicles. (The pigs, several of whom possessed more than one vehicle, also required an expanded access to parking facilities.)

For the most part, the animals who were left behind on Foxwood and Pinchfield made for a ready supply of laborers, valet parkers, security guards, outhouse cleaners, and groundskeepers. The franchise, Duncan Dognuts, had been introduced to provide the local work forces with the required nutrients. It was fortunate their needs were limited, as their disposable income, being equal to their skills, was also limited. Really, those animals were lucky to have jobs at all. Many, who were totally useless, didn't.

The pigs, naturally, could not allow any farming on the undeveloped portions of the two farms—because it had not been preapproved. So the dogs were charged with keeping a constant eye on the animals that Frederick and Pilkington had deemed too worthless to relocate, as the freeloaders among them were always planting beds of carrots and radishes—heaven knows for what reason. A few of the more educated Foxwood and Pinchfield animals were permitted to take up permanent residence on Animal Fair—there was a cow with a knowledge of cheese-making, and a horse with an excellent background in military maneuvers, and several geese that could sort grain—but the unemployable undesirables . . . well, they were just left to whatever fate they had made for themselves. Although periodically called upon to dig out an old latrine or bury a carcass too festering to keep on display, for the most part, they were kept off in the various patches of weeds on the outskirts of the parking lots. Out of sight was really the best place for them anyway, as they were not much to look at—a few sheep who were forced to shear each other (with crude results), a gone-dry cow, a litter of snot-nosed puppies, a three-legged cat, et cetera. . . . After all, not everyone could have a tub. And from the way those wretched animals allowed themselves to smell, it was supposed, not everyone would want one.

Few of the fair animals could even imagine life without hot showers.

And yet, as easy as it was to find a hot shower, there did seem to be a few odd goings-on around the fair. The termites were proliferating at a rate beyond anything heretofore combated. And there were, too, the woodpecker holes, which seemed to be everywhere. Hobart the bull, upon a visit to the carnival, suggested they might be beaver holes—though that idea was quickly proven incorrect by the *Trotter*. As for the wild onions that had sprouted in the grass lawns—well, the animals just gazed at them, and ate at the stalks off-pawdedly, and burped, and passed gas, and wondered distantly about that unpleasant whiff of onion.

And for all that, the warm sunny days still came — one after another. And the animals of Animal Fair went about their lives and labors.

And it was on one sunny summer Tuesday, not especially anything exceptional, that the lives of the animals would be changed forever. . . .

Their livelihoods, and even their existence, would be thrown into question — the future, so solid and impervious the day before, would become newly uncertain. It would be as if the comfortable days of the past had sought their own compensation — and where yesterday had been secure, tomorrow would be perilous.

And indeed, all was imperiled, on that Tuesday.

The ticket-takers had opened the gates of the park only a few minutes before . . . and the park visitors (each one a good, paying customer) sallied forth to the games, exhibits, or rides of their choice . . . and the park workers toted coffee and croissants to their places of occupation . . .

And it happened.

The Ferris Wheel was one of the major attractions of the park. Placed at the top of the second hill of the fairgrounds, the massive structure whirled with surprising speed — and from high atop, there was a spectacular view of the Twin Mills on the next hill, and the village across the road. By the end of the day, the lines grew long, prohibitively so, but in the morning hour, anyone could meander up the short ramp, and, with his or her partner, occupy one of the dozen cabs on the wheel.

And on this morning, a crowd of Woodlands rabbits, geese, and squirrels had been the first to the Ferris Wheel. And with the woolen candy salesman calling out his wares, and the warmth of the sun cutting through the dissipating mist of dawn, the Ferris Wheel made its first slow revolution—and then began accelerating. A ferret, who had explained he had acrophobia, stood with the Ferris Wheel operator, a poodle named Arthur, who had retired from jumping through flaming hoops.

"Higher, higher! Faster, faster!" chanted the ferret.

And then, in a sudden slicing motion of the paw—it all began.

It would later be argued as to whether the evildoers had secured preplaced weaponry from a passing peanut cart, or had foiled the bloodhounds by dousing themselves and their arsenal in apple-wood oil, in order to mask any tell-tale odor. But regardless of the method that his treachery had taken, this ferret's time had come. . . .

He had drawn his blade, cut the throat of Arthur the poodle, and assumed the controls of the Ferris Wheel—and before anyone could understand what was happening (was it part of the ride?) the Ferris Wheel had accelerated to its top speed. Gears ground. Sparks flew. And two pairs of squirrels were dragging paper bags through the ironwork—up to the axle that held the wheel in place. And then, in a moment horrifyingly lucid, the squirrels doused themselves with some greasy liquid, and set themselves on fire. The bags exploded, and the Ferris Wheel was loosed—kicked from its moorings.

And the crowds of Animal Fair watched in a static horror as the wheel rolled, unstoppably, down the one hill, up the other . . . and towards the waiting Twin Mills.

Some of the animals on the ground were crying out in terror —and some of the animals on the Ferris Wheel were crying out as well. From the highest of the cabs, one human father was shouting down to his two sons, who had not met the height requirement, and to his wife, who had remained with the boys—

"I love you. Goodbye. I love you."

Other voices began screaming—other bodies began running.

There was a putrid black smoke in the air—the corpses of the squirrels were now burning by their own fat. There were other animals—riding the Ferris Wheel—who were evidently part of the attack. With fanatical glee, they were shaking their fists and screeching—

"The Sugarcandy Lodestar!"

"The Sugarcandy Lodestar!"

And with that, the fair animals remembered Moses—and his Sugarcandy tales. And as they ran and took cover, they thought—perhaps therein lay some clue.

At the fair, it had been long agreed that if some fool duck or frog was so backwards as to give high-standing to Moses— well then, so be it, as the farm had Moses, and the likes of his paltry, miserable followers, well in hoof. But now, and suddenly so, Moses's followers were returned to that lofty status that many had yet to experience in their own lifetimes. And they were elevated not just for the stressful occasion, as that was typically when interest in Sugarcandy Mountain soared, but because those fair animals who followed Moses had some idea as to what those fool squirrels were screeching about. And even if Moses himself was nowhere to be seen, the Animal Fair followers of Moses were swift to provide his insight. Well versed in his preachings (for trials just such as this) they had immediately perceived the mistake in doctrine. It was that loathsome misinterpretation they had seen before. And as they especially hated any purveyors of this so wrongheaded notion of the Sugarcandy Lodestar—so totally at odds with the divine revelation of the Sugarcandy Mountain—they made the correction quite vehemently.

"No, no! It's not the Sugarcandy Lodestar! It's the Sugarcandy Mountain!"

And as they said it—the Ferris Wheel rolled into the Twin Mills.

And as they said it—each of the cabs occupied by the fanatical Woodlands animals began exploding and burning.

The woolen candy concession stand, which had been in the path of the Ferris Wheel, was outright flattened—and in a flash, it was aflame. The thick black mulch in the air dropped everyone to the ground—to roll, to gag, to choke.

Flames of woolen candy fell from the sky. The fire stuck to fur and flesh—and those seared made a sound nobody ever wanted to hear again.

Then, the first of the Twin Mills, which had taken the brunt of the force of the Ferris Wheel . . . it collapsed. With a crash that shuttled several of the chickens into the air, all that labor, all that lavished labor, was reduced to a dust—an unbreathable, black, killing dust.

In the cloud of the mills, there was no sight other than the forms of flaming animals jumping from the windows—and plummeting into the fiery rubble below.

But—it wasn't over. More screams, more broken bodies—and one of the bumper cars had driven out of its tire-walled enclosure, and into the park. Swerving, tipping on its wheels, the car veered towards the laboratory of Thomas the goat. (Was Thomas inside?) With a mad yell, the driver of the car, a white and brown rabbit with huge, bulging, pink eyes, careened into the structure—

"The Beaver Code forever!"

The beavers! The animals realized—it was the beavers! The believers in Sugarcandy Mountain had been right! It was those crazed beavers and their stupid Lodestar! They were the ones!

Even if they were nowhere to be seen—they were the ones! They were the ones, even if, now, they were embodied by only a pawful of crazed frogs, rabbits—and one elderly mole. All with big, rounded eyes, they shouted through the smoke—

"Free the village from the pigs!"

A hedgehog riding one of the horses screamed it louder than the others—

"Free the village!"

The three horses, who could only recite the alphabet to the letter B, made up the Horsey Ride, which mostly catered to juvenile animals who had visited the park with their parents. Only the occasional adult would ride the horses, who were agreeable even when they were required to bear the heavier load, as they had been allowed to name the ride "Clover's Horsey Ride," after the mare who had watched over them, and loved them, even though they were dumb, when they were mere foals.

But now, they were foals no longer—they were enormous, powerful animals. And one of them had broken away. Having jumped the fence that surrounded the Horsey track, one of the three brutes was charging—running erratically through the fires. The animals were bawling desperately to the horse— trying to explain to him that the hedgehog on his back was the enemy. But that big dumb horse was galloping—and there's no explaining anything to a big dumb horse galloping.

And if there was no stopping that charge, the only thing left to do was save the lives of any animals that might be in the path of (or a part of) that hedgehog's target. *What is the target?* The way the horse and hedgehog ran helter-skelter, it was nearly impossible to tell if they were actually headed in any direction. But, whatever direction, whatever target, one could see that it, whatever it was, was coming up, as the hedgehog, opening his backpack (presumably packed with gunpowder), was dousing himself and the horse with kerosene poured from a thermos. He held the lighter in his paw.

It was only Benjamin the donkey who could see, or thought he could see, the hedgehog's intentions. The pigs and goats, apparently, feared that the Jones House was the hedgehog's target—but Benjamin saw differently. Wherever that hedgehog meant to go, that horse was taking him directly to the new barracks—Thomas Towers. A nervous horse, Benjamin knew it, would always go home.

And in that barracks, Benjamin also knew, there were at least a hundred animals—some sleeping, some just sitting around on their four-day weekend. And among those animals, sleeping in Benjamin's very own stall, was the love of his life, the one love of his life, the one love of his life that he had waited through youth and middle-age to find—Emerald the mathematical donkey. Emerald and her son, Kip, of whom Benjamin had also grown quite fond.

And Benjamin . . . who had always told the animals of the fair that they would never see how a donkey died, realized his mistake. He had said a thousand times that they would never see him die—but now, he knew, he was wrong. He had been wrong before—not to care, not to have hope—and now, he was wrong again. Donkeys lived a long, long time—but for all, even a donkey, an end would come. And this, for Benjamin, was the end.

"Now," bayed Benjamin, not so much to anyone in partic-ular as to the world he was bidding good-bye, "You see how a donkey dies!"

Benjamin thought—

Kip and Emerald, they're young, and I'm old. And there are other young animals in that new barn. And I know it wouldn't have mattered to me much a year ago, or five years ago, or ten years ago—but it isn't fair a short, cruel life gets shorter and crueler.

"Now you see how a donkey dies!"

And even as Benjamin issued forth those words to posterity, he was already running towards the spiny hedgehog on the rampaging cart-horse. And just as the pair erupted into flames, Benjamin's body collided into them. And the three toppled, and burned—in a grotesque heap between the Jones House and the new barracks. And as their blazing limbs still flimmered, and a unified pain screamed from the pile of three—those who were still alive knew that no one else would perish there. . . .

Benjamin, who had been asked a million questions, had finally found the answer. Benjamin, who had lived a million days, had finally found the one thing that could make him alive. Benjamin, that defeated, cynical, heart-broken donkey, had discovered that love, for Emerald, for Kip, for all the animals of the fair, was the meaning of his life. And then, to save their lives, Benjamin had given his own.

Benjamin had died a hero, and for those who saw, they would tell . . . that was how a donkey died.

Transfixed by the catastrophe, animals watched as a vast cloud of smoke engulfed the day. And suddenly, it was night. A moonless, starless night. A night—not of a setting sun, but of a rising blackness. Animals on two legs fell to all fours, and some, from there, fell to their bellies—to gasp the black breaths that would be their last. In an instant, they were covered, buried, and lost.

Amidst flames and frenzy out of control, a gone-wild gray squirrel—a feral, ferocious Woodlands animal—screamed the Beaver Creed as he was shaken to death by a dog.

Through the killing smoke, sheep wheezed angrily—
"The Woodlands animals! The Woodlands animals!"
And dogs arriving on the scene repeated them—
"The Woodlands animals! The Woodlands animals!"

And one of the shepherds nabbed a running rabbit. Wasn't that Zeke? The Woodland newcomer who worked the candy-apple stand? And before any animal could formulate a word, or even a thought, that dog had torn Zeke to shreds. And that dog—anyone who looked at that dog immediately saw it—he must have known something about Zeke the rabbit. And to look at Zeke—well, even in a chaos like this, he was clearly guilty of something.

And one couldn't help but realize—not even the sheep needed it explained—every Woodlands animal was a conspirator.

"Where are the Woodlands animals? The Woodlands animals?" asked the dogs. "Have you seen any beavers? Student beavers?" And the fair animals pointed to where the Woodlands animals, all of them recent immigrants, had taken shelter. And the fair animals pointed to where the beavers, and the student beavers, had taken shelter. And the dogs, in their clenched jaws, dragged the Woodlands creatures away. . . .

And then came the goats—breaking out gas masks from large crates that had appeared from somewhere. And as the goats were already wearing the masks, no animal could tell one goat from another. Who was who? Were they their goats? Was Thomas still alive to protect them?

Yes, the animals could see as the dogs donned the masks, these were their goats. They were good goats!

And after the dogs had adjusted the head straps of their own masks (the pigs were already snug in theirs), they distributed them to the hysterical fair animals, who were either running to and fro, not knowing where to go, or just standing, frozen in fear. And as the dogs passed out the masks, the goats were saying, "There's nothing to worry about, it's not dangerous. Just stay where you are." And the dogs were repeating, "There's nothing to worry about, it's not dangerous. Just stay where you are." And the animals were doing just that, and as the second Twin Mill collapsed on them—they died where they stood.

And more dust rose—and there was blackness. And then there was Snowball, standing atop the chicken coop.

And the animals heard that great pig Snowball, who had somehow acquired a bullhorn, announcing, "We were prepared for this." And without pause, that great pig Snowball called the extremist attack, "The Massacre of the Twin Mills." And for it, he vowed—

"Revenge, justice, retaliation! The blood of beavers will flow in the river of the Woodlands!"

And from the rowdiest of the badgers and geese to the most retiring of the voles and ducks—all the animals were calling out for this deliverance. They foamed at the maw and the beak—and the fangs of dogs pointed through an angry froth. And the divisions of shepherds pouring forth from the Jones House were more fierce and multitudinous than anyone could have ever imagined. And the animals, they received the legions of dogs with heartfelt cheers—and feathers and fur raised in vengeance. They were all big now.

The sheep started out with something they had retained from somewhere—

"It's entirely up to us! It's entirely up to us."

And in only a moment their coarse cheer had overcome itself with that roar more rousing and familiar—

"Animal Fair! Animal Fair!"

And the rest of the park animals, who were usually silenced by such outbursts from the sheep, this time responded, belting out a battle cry of their own—one that quickly overpowered the baa-ing of the sheep altogether.

"Kill the beavers!"

"Kill the beavers!"

"Kill!"

"Kill!"

"Kill!"

ROOF BOOKS

- Andrews, Bruce. **EX WHY ZEE.** 112p. $10.95.
- Andrews, Bruce. **Getting Ready To Have Been Frightened**. 116p. $7.50.
- Benson, Steve. **Blue Book**. Copub. with The Figures. 250p. $12.50
- Bernstein, Charles. **Islets/Irritations**. 112p. $9.95.
- Bernstein, Charles (editor). **The Politics of Poetic Form**. 246p. $12.95; cloth $21.95.
- Brossard, Nicole. **Picture Theory**. 188p. $11.95.
- Champion, Miles. **Three Bell Zero**. 72p. $10.95.
- Child, Abigail. **Scatter Matrix**. 79p. $9.95.
- Davies, Alan. **Active 24 Hours**. 100p. $5.
- Davies, Alan. **Signage**. 184p. $11.
- Davies, Alan. **Rave**. 64p. $7.95.
- Day, Jean. **A Young Recruit**. 58p. $6.
- Di Palma, Ray. **Motion of the Cypher**. 112p. $10.95.
- Di Palma, Ray. **Raik**. 100p. $9.95.
- Doris, Stacy. **Kildare**. 104p. $9.95.
- Dreyer, Lynne. **The White Museum**. 80p. $6.
- Edwards, Ken. **Good Science.** 80p. $9.95.
- Eigner, Larry. **Areas Lights Heights**. 182p. $12, $22 (cloth).
- Gizzi, Michael. **Continental Harmonies**. 92p. $8.95.
- Goldman, Judith. **Vocoder**. 96p. $11.95.
- Gottlieb, Michael. **Ninety-Six Tears**. 88p. $5.
- Gottlieb, Michael. **Gorgeous Plunge**. 96p. $11.95.
- Greenwald, Ted. **Jumping the Line**. 120p. $12.95.
- Grenier, Robert. **A Day at the Beach**. 80p. $6.
- Grosman, Ernesto. **The XULReader: An Anthology of Argentine Poetry (1981–1996)**. 167p. $14.95.
- Hills, Henry. **Making Money**. 72p. $7.50. VHS video $24.95. Book & tape $29.95.
- Huang Yunte. **SHI: A Radical Reading of Chinese Poetry.** 76p. $9.95
- Hunt, Erica. **Local History**. 80 p. $9.95.
- Kuszai, Joel (editor) **poetics@**, 192 p. $13.95.
- Inman, P. **Criss Cross**. 64 p. $7.95.
- Inman, P. **Red Shift**. 64p. $6.
- Lazer, Hank. **Doublespace**. 192 p. $12.
- Levy, Andrew. **Paper Head Last Lyrics**. 112 p. $11.95.

- Mac Low, Jackson. **Representative Works: 1938–1985**. 360p. $12.95, $18.95 (cloth).
- Mac Low, Jackson. **Twenties**. 112p. $8.95.
- Moriarty, Laura. **Rondeaux**. 107p. $8.
- Neilson, Melanie. **Civil Noir**. 96p. $8.95.
- Pearson, Ted. **Planetary Gear**. 72p. $8.95.
- Perelman, Bob. **Virtual Reality**. 80p. $9.95.
- Perelman, Bob. **The Future of Memory.** 120p. $14.95.
- Piombino, Nick, **The Boundary of Blur**. 128p. $13.95.
- Raworth, Tom. **Clean & Will-Lit**. 106p. $10.95.
- Robins, Corinne. **Marble Goddesses with Technicolor Skins.** 112p. $11.95.
- Robinson, Kit. **Balance Sheet.** 112p. $11.95.
- Robinson, Kit. **Democracy Boulevard.** 104p. $9.95.
- Robinson, Kit. **Ice Cubes**. 96p. $6.
- Rosenfield, Kim. **Good Morning — Midnight**. 112p. $10.95.
- Scalapino, Leslie. **Objects in the Terrifying Tense Longing from Taking Place.** 88p. $9.95.
- Seaton, Peter. **The Son Master**. 64p. $5.
- Shaw, Lytle. **The Lobe**. 80p. $11.95.
- Sherry, James. **Popular Fiction**. 84p. $6.
- Silliman, Ron. **The New Sentence**. 200p. $10.
- Silliman, Ron. **N/O**. 112p. $10.95.
- Smith, Rod. **Protective Immediacy**. 96p. $9.95
- Stefans, Brian Kim. **Free Space Comix**.
- Tarkos, Christophe. **Ma Langue est Poétique—Selected Works**. 96p. $12.95.
- Templeton, Fiona. **Cells of Release**. 128p. with photographs. $13.95.
- Templeton, Fiona. **YOU—The City**. 150p. $11.95.
- Torres, Edwin. **The All-Union Day of the Shock Worker**. 112p. $10.95.
- Ward, Diane. **Human Ceiling**. 80p. $8.95.
- Ward, Diane. **Relation**. 64p. $7.50.
- Watson, Craig. **Free Will**. 80p. $9.95.
- Watten, Barrett. **Progress**. 122p. $7.50.
- Weiner, Hannah. **We Speak Silent**. 76 p. $9.95
- Wellman, Mac. **Miniature**. 112 p. $12.95
- Wolsak, Lissa. **Pen Chants**. 80p. $9.95.
- Yasusada, Araki. **Doubled Flowering: From the Notebooks of Araki Yasusada.** 272p. $14.95.

ROOF BOOKS
are published by
Segue Foundation, 303 East 8th Street, New York, NY 10009
Visit our website at segue.org

Roof Books are distributed by
SMALL PRESS DISTRIBUTION
1341 Seventh Avenue, Berkeley, CA. 94710-1403.
Phone orders: 800-869-7553
spdbooks.org